THE TREES OF PRIDE

THE TREES OF PRIDE

G. K. CHESTERTON

Serenity
Publishers, LLC

ROCKVILLE, MARYLAND

2009

ISBN: 978-1-60450-690-7

Published by Serenity Publishers
An Arc Manor Company
P. O. Box 10339
Rockville, MD 20849-0339
www.SerenityPublishers.com

Printed in the United States of America/United Kingdom

CONTENTS

I. THE TALE OF THE PEACOCK TREES

Squire Vane was an elderly schoolboy of English education and Irish extraction. His English education, at one of the great public schools, had preserved his intellect perfectly and permanently at the stage of boyhood. But his Irish extraction subconsciously upset in him the proper solemnity of an old boy, and sometimes gave him back the brighter outlook of a naughty boy. He had a bodily impatience which played tricks upon him almost against his will, and had already rendered him rather too radiant a failure in civil and diplomatic service. Thus it is true that compromise is the key of British policy, especially as effecting an impartiality among the religions of India; but Vane's attempt to meet the Moslem halfway by kicking off one boot at the gates of the mosque, was felt not so much to indicate true impartiality as something that could only be called an aggressive indifference. Again, it is true that an English aristocrat can hardly enter fully into the feelings of either party in a quarrel between a Russian Jew and an Orthodox procession carrying relics; but Vane's idea that the procession might carry the Jew as well, himself a venerable and historic relic, was misunderstood on both sides. In short, he was a man who particularly prided himself on having no nonsense about him; with the result that he was always doing nonsensical things. He seemed to be standing on his head merely to prove that he was hard-headed.

He had just finished a hearty breakfast, in the society of his daughter, at a table under a tree in his garden by the Cornish coast. For, having a glorious circulation, he insisted on as many outdoor meals as possible, though spring had barely touched the woods and warmed the seas round that southern extremity of England. His daughter Barbara, a good-looking girl with heavy red hair and a face as grave as one of the garden statues, still sat almost motionless as a statue when her father rose. A fine tall figure in light clothes, with his white hair and mustache flying backwards rather fiercely from a face that was good-humored enough, for he carried his very wide Panama hat in his hand, he strode across the terraced garden, down some stone steps flanked with old ornamental urns to a more woodland path fringed with little trees, and so down a zigzag road which descended the craggy Cliff to the shore, where he was to meet a guest arriving by boat. A yacht was already in the blue bay, and he could see a boat pulling toward the little paved pier.

And yet in that short walk between the green turf and the yellow sands he was destined to find, his hard-headedness provoked into a not unfamiliar phase which the world was inclined to call hot-headedness. The fact was that the Cornish peasantry, who composed his tenantry and domestic establishment, were far from being people with no nonsense about them. There was, alas! a great deal of nonsense about them; with ghosts, witches, and traditions as old as Merlin, they seemed to surround him with a fairy ring of nonsense. But the magic circle had one center: there was one point in which the curving conversation of the rustics always returned. It was a point that always pricked the Squire to exasperation, and even in this short walk he seemed to strike it everywhere. He paused before descending the steps from the lawn to speak to the gardener about potting some foreign shrubs, and the gardener seemed to be gloomily gratified, in every line of his leathery brown visage, at the chance of indicating that he had formed a low opinion of foreign shrubs.

"We wish you'd get rid of what you've got here, sir," he observed, digging doggedly. "Nothing'll grow right with them here."

"Shrubs!" said the Squire, laughing. "You don't call the peacock trees shrubs, do you? Fine tall trees—you ought to be proud of them."

"Ill weeds grow apace," observed the gardener. "Weeds can grow as houses when somebody plants them." Then he added: "Him that sowed tares in the Bible, Squire."

"Oh, blast your—" began the Squire, and then replaced the more apt and alliterative word "Bible" by the general word "superstition." He was himself a robust rationalist, but he went to church to set his tenants an example. Of what, it would have puzzled him to say.

A little way along the lower path by the trees he encountered a woodcutter, one Martin, who was more explicit, having more of a grievance. His daughter was at that time seriously ill with a fever recently common on that coast, and the Squire, who was a kind-hearted gentleman, would normally have made allowances for low spirits and loss of temper. But he came near to losing his own again when the peasant persisted in connecting his tragedy with the traditional monomania about the foreign trees.

"If she were well enough I'd move her," said the woodcutter, "as we can't move them, I suppose. I'd just like to get my chopper into them and feel 'em come crashing down."

"One would think they were dragons," said Vane.

"And that's about what they look like," replied Martin. "Look at 'em!"

The woodman was naturally a rougher and even wilder figure than the gardener. His face also was brown, and looked like an antique parchment, and it was framed in an outlandish arrangement of raven beard and whiskers, which was really a fashion fifty years ago, but might have been five thousand years old or older. Phoenicians, one felt, trading on those strange shores in the morning of the world, might have combed or curled or braided their blue-black hair into some such quaint patterns.

For this patch of population was as much a corner of Cornwall as Cornwall is a corner of England; a tragic and unique race, small and interrelated like a Celtic clan. The clan was older than the Vane family, though that was old as county families go. For in many such parts of England it is the aristocrats who are the latest arrivals. It was the sort of racial type that is supposed to be passing, and perhaps has already passed.

The obnoxious objects stood some hundred yards away from the speaker, who waved toward them with his ax; and there was something suggestive in the comparison. That coast, to begin with, stretching toward the sunset, was itself almost as fantastic as a sunset cloud. It was cut out against the emerald or indigo of the sea in graven horns and crescents that might be the cast or mold of some such crested serpents; and, beneath, was pierced and fretted by caves and crevices, as if by the boring of some such titanic worms. Over and above this draconian architecture of the earth a veil of gray woods hung thinner like a vapor; woods which the witchcraft of the sea had, as usual, both blighted and blown out of shape. To the right the trees trailed along the sea front in a single line, each drawn out in thin wild lines like a caricature. At the other end of their extent they multiplied into a huddle of hunchbacked trees, a wood spreading toward a projecting part of the high coast. It was here that the sight appeared to which so many eyes and minds seemed to be almost automatically turning.

Out of the middle of this low, and more or less level wood, rose three separate stems that shot up and soared into the sky like a lighthouse out of the waves or a church spire out of the village roofs. They formed a clump of three columns close together, which might well be the mere bifurcation, or rather trifurcation, of one tree, the lower part being lost or sunken in the thick wood around. Everything about them suggested something stranger and more southern than anything even in that last peninsula of Britain which pushes out farthest toward Spain and Africa and the southern stars. Their leathery leafage had sprouted in advance of the faint mist of yellow-green around them, and it was of another and less natural green, tinged with blue, like the colors of a kingfisher. But one might fancy it the scales of some three-headed dragon towering over a herd of huddled and fleeing cattle.

"I am exceedingly sorry your girl is so unwell," said Vane shortly. "But really—" and he strode down the steep road with plunging strides.

The boat was already secured to the little stone jetty, and the boatman, a younger shadow of the woodcutter—and, indeed, a nephew of that useful malcontent—saluted his territorial lord with the sullen formality of the family. The Squire acknowledged it casually and had soon forgotten all such things in shaking hands with the visitor who had just come ashore. The visitor was a long, loose man, very lean to be so young, whose long, fine features seemed wholly fitted together of bone and nerve, and seemed somehow to contrast with his hair, that showed in vivid yellow patches upon his hollow temples under the brim of his white holiday hat. He was carefully dressed in exquisite taste, though he had come straight from a considerable sea voyage; and he carried something in his hand which in his long European travels, and even longer European visits, he had almost forgotten to call a gripsack.

Mr. Cyprian Paynter was an American who lived in Italy. There was a good deal more to be said about him, for he was a very acute and cultivated gentleman; but those two facts would, perhaps, cover most of the others. Storing his mind like a museum with the wonder of the Old World, but all lit up as by a window with the wonder of the New, he had fallen heir to some thing of the unique critical position of Ruskin or Pater, and was further famous as a discoverer of minor poets. He was a judicious discoverer, and he did not turn all his minor poets into major prophets. If his geese were swans, they were not all Swans of Avon. He had even incurred the deadly suspicion of classicism by differing from his young friends, the Punctuist Poets, when they produced versification consisting exclusively of commas and colons. He had a more humane sympathy with the modern flame kindled from the embers of Celtic mythology, and it was in reality the recent appearance of a Cornish poet, a sort of parallel to the new Irish poets, which had brought him on this occasion to Cornwall. He was, indeed, far too well-mannered to allow a host to guess that any pleasure was being sought outside his own hospitality. He had a long standing invitation from Vane, whom he had met in Cyprus in the latter's days of undiplomatic diplomacy; and Vane was not aware that relations had only been thus renewed after the critic had read Merlin and Other Verses, by a new writer named John Treherne. Nor did the Squire even begin to realize the much more diplomatic diplomacy by which he had been induced to invite the local bard to lunch on the very day of the American critic's arrival.

Mr. Paynter was still standing with his gripsack, gazing in a trance of true admiration at the hollowed crags, topped by the gray, grotesque wood, and crested finally by the three fantastic trees.

"It is like being shipwrecked on the coast of fairyland," he said,

"I hope you haven't been shipwrecked much," replied his host, smiling. "I fancy Jake here can look after you very well."

Mr. Paynter looked across at the boatman and smiled also. "I am afraid," he said, "our friend is not quite so enthusiastic for this landscape as I am."

"Oh, the trees, I suppose!" said the Squire wearily.

The boatman was by normal trade a fisherman; but as his house, built of black tarred timber, stood right on the foreshore a few yards from the pier, he was employed in such cases as a sort of ferryman. He was a big, black-browed youth generally silent, but something seemed now to sting him into speech.

"Well, sir," he said, "everybody knows it's not natural. Everybody knows the sea blights trees and beats them under, when they're only just trees. These things thrive like some unholy great seaweed that don't belong to the land at all. It's like the—the blessed sea serpent got on shore, Squire, and eating everything up."

"There is some stupid legend," said Squire Vane gruffly. "But come up into the garden; I want to introduce you to my daughter."

When, however, they reached the little table under the tree, the apparently immovable young lady had moved away after all, and it was some time before they came upon the track of her. She had risen, though languidly, and wandered slowly along the upper path of the terraced garden looking down on the lower path where it ran closer to the main bulk of the little wood by the sea.

Her languor was not a feebleness but rather a fullness of life, like that of a child half awake; she seemed to stretch herself and enjoy everything without noticing anything. She passed the wood, into the gray huddle of which a single white path vanished through a black hole. Along this part of the terrace ran something like a low rampart or balustrade, embowered with flowers at intervals; and she leaned over it, looking down at another glimpse of the glowing sea behind the clump of trees, and on another irregular path tumbling down to the pier and the boatman's cottage on the beach.

As she gazed, sleepily enough, she saw that a strange figure was very actively climbing the path, apparently coming from the fisherman's cottage; so actively that a moment afterwards it came out between the trees and stood upon the path just below her. It was not only a figure strange to her, but one somewhat strange in itself. It was that of a man still young, and seeming somehow younger than his own clothes, which were not only shabby but antiquated; clothes common enough in texture, yet carried in an uncommon fashion. He wore what was presumably a light waterproof, perhaps through having come off the sea; but it was held at the throat by one button, and hung, sleeves and all, more like a cloak than a coat. He rested one bony hand on a black stick; under the shadow of his broad hat his black hair hung down in a tuft or two. His face, which was swarthy, but rather handsome in itself, wore something that may have been a slightly embarrassed smile, but had too much the appearance of a sneer.

Whether this apparition was a tramp or a trespasser, or a friend of some of the fishers or woodcutters, Barbara Vane was quite unable to guess. He removed his hat, still with his unaltered and rather sinister smile, and said civilly: "Excuse me. The Squire asked me to call." Here he caught sight of Martin, the woodman, who was shifting along the path, thinning the thin trees; and the stranger made a familiar salute with one finger.

The girl did not know what to say. "Have you—have you come about cutting the wood?" she asked at last.

"I would I were so honest a man," replied the stranger. "Martin is, I fancy, a distant cousin of mine; we Cornish folk just round here are nearly all related, you know; but I do not cut wood. I do not cut anything, except, perhaps, capers. I am, so to speak, a jongleur."

"A what?" asked Barbara.

"A minstrel, shall we say?" answered the newcomer, and looked up at her more steadily. During a rather odd silence their eyes rested on each other. What she saw has been already noted, though by her, at any rate, not in the least understood. What he saw was a decidedly beautiful woman with a statuesque face and hair that shone in the sun like a helmet of copper.

"Do you know," he went on, "that in this old place, hundreds of years ago, a jongleur may really have stood where I stand, and a lady may really have looked over that wall and thrown him money?"

"Do you want money?" she asked, all at sea.

"Well," drawled the stranger, "in the sense of lacking it, perhaps, but I fear there is no place now for a minstrel, except nigger minstrel. I must apologize for not blacking my face."

She laughed a little in her bewilderment, and said: "Well, I hardly think you need do that."

"You think the natives here are dark enough already, perhaps," he observed calmly. "After all, we are aborigines, and are treated as such."

She threw out some desperate remark about the weather or the scenery, and wondered what would happen next.

"The prospect is certainly beautiful," he assented, in the same enigmatic manner. "There is only one thing in it I am doubtful about."

While she stood in silence he slowly lifted his black stick like a long black finger and pointed it at the peacock trees above the wood. And a queer feeling of disquiet fell on the girl, as if he were, by that mere gesture, doing a destructive act and could send a blight upon the garden.

The strained and almost painful silence was broken by the voice of Squire Vane, loud even while it was still distant.

"We couldn't make out where you'd got to, Barbara," he said. "This is my friend, Mr. Cyprian Paynter." The next moment he saw the stranger and stopped, a little puzzled. It was only Mr. Cyprian Paynter himself who was equal to the situation. He had seen months ago a portrait of the new Cornish poet in some American literary magazine, and he found himself, to his surprise, the introducer instead of the introduced.

"Why, Squire," he said in considerable astonishment, "don't you know Mr. Treherne? I supposed, of course, he was a neighbor."

"Delighted to see you, Mr. Treherne," said the Squire, recovering his manners with a certain genial confusion. "So pleased you were able to come. This is Mr. Paynter—my daughter," and, turning with a certain boisterous embarrassment, he led the way to the table under the tree.

Cyprian Paynter followed, inwardly revolving a puzzle which had taken even his experience by surprise. The American, if intellectually an aristocrat, was still socially and subconsciously a democrat. It had never crossed his mind that the poet should be counted lucky to know the squire and not the squire to know the poet. The honest patronage in Vane's hospitality was something which made Paynter feel he was, after all, an exile in England.

The Squire, anticipating the trial of luncheon with a strange literary man, had dealt with the case tactfully from his own standpoint. County society might have made the guest feel like a fish out of water; and, except for the American critic and the local lawyer and doctor, worthy middle-class people who fitted into the picture, he had kept it as a family party. He was a widower, and when the meal had been laid out on the garden table, it was Barbara who presided as hostess. She had the new poet on her right hand and it made her very uncomfortable. She had practically offered that fallacious jongleur money, and it did not make it easier to offer him lunch.

"The whole countryside's gone mad," announced the Squire, by way of the latest local news. "It's about this infernal legend of ours."

"I collect legends," said Paynter, smiling.

"You must remember I haven't yet had a chance to collect yours. And this," he added, looking round at the romantic coast, "is a fine theater for anything dramatic."

"Oh, it's dramatic in its way," admitted Vane, not without a faint satisfaction. "It's all about those things over there we call the peacock trees—I suppose, because of the queer color of the leaf, you know, though I have heard they make a shrill noise in a high wind that's supposed to be like the shriek of a peacock; something like a bamboo in the botanical structure, perhaps. Well, those trees are supposed to have been brought over from Barbary by my ancestor Sir Walter Vane, one of the Elizabethan patriots or pirates, or whatever you call them. They say that at the end of his last voyage the villagers gathered on the beach down there and saw the boat standing in from the sea, and the new trees stood up in the boat like a mast, all gay with leaves out of season, like green bunting. And as they watched they thought at first that the boat was steering oddly, and then that it wasn't steering at all; and when it drifted to the shore at last every man in that boat was dead, and Sir Walter Vane, with his sword drawn, was leaning up against the tree trunk, as stiff as the tree."

"Now this is rather curious," remarked Paynter thoughtfully. "I told you I collected legends, and I fancy I can tell you the beginning of the story of which that is the end, though it comes hundreds of miles across the sea."

He tapped meditatively on the table with his thin, taper fingers, like a man trying to recall a tune. He had, indeed, made a hobby of such fables, and he was not without vanity about his artistic touch in telling them.

"Oh, do tell us your part of it?" cried Barbara Vane, whose air of sunny sleepiness seemed in some vague degree to have fallen from her.

The American bowed across the table with a serious politeness, and then began playing idly with a quaint ring on his long finger as he talked.

"If you go down to the Barbary Coast, where the last wedge of the forest narrows down between the desert and the great tideless sea, you will find the natives still telling a strange story about a saint of the Dark Ages. There, on the twilight border of the Dark Continent, you feel the Dark Ages. I have only visited the place once, though it lies, so to speak, opposite to the Italian city where I lived for years, and yet you would hardly believe how the topsy-turvydom and transmigration of this myth somehow seemed less mad than they really are, with the wood loud with lions at night and that dark red solitude beyond. They say that the hermit St. Securis, living there among trees, grew to love them like companions; since, though great giants with many arms like Briareus, they were the mildest and most blameless of the creatures; they did not devour like the lions, but rather opened their arms to all the little birds. And he prayed that they might be loosened from time to time to walk like other things. And the trees were moved upon the prayers of Securis, as they were at the songs of Orpheus. The men of the desert were stricken from afar with fear, seeing the saint walking with a walking grove, like a schoolmaster with his boys. For the trees were thus freed under strict conditions of discipline. They were to return at the sound of the hermit's bell, and, above all, to copy the wild beasts in walking only to destroy and devour nothing. Well, it is said that one of the trees heard a voice that was not the saint's; that in the warm green twilight of one summer evening it became conscious of some thing sitting and speaking in its branches in the guise of a great bird, and it was that which once spoke from a tree in the guise of a great serpent. As the voice grew louder among its murmuring leaves the tree was torn with a great desire to stretch out and snatch at the birds that flew harmlessly about their nests, and pluck them to pieces. Finally, the tempter filled the tree-top with his own birds of pride, the starry pageant of the peacocks. And the spirit of the brute overcame the spirit of the tree, and it rent and consumed the blue-green birds till not a plume was left, and returned to the quiet tribe of trees. But they say that when spring came all the other trees put forth leaves, but this put forth feathers of a strange hue and pattern. And by that monstrous assimilation the saint knew of the sin, and he rooted that one tree to the earth with a judgment, so that evil should fall on any who re-moved it again. That, Squire, is the beginning in the deserts of the tale that ended here, almost in this garden."

"And the end is about as reliable as the beginning, I should say," said Vane. "Yours is a nice plain tale for a small tea-party; a quiet little bit of still-life, that is."

"What a queer, horrible story," exclaimed Barbara. "It makes one feel like a cannibal."

"Ex Africa," said the lawyer, smiling. "It comes from a cannibal country. I think it's the touch of the tar-brush, that nightmare feeling that you don't know whether the hero is a plant or a man or a devil. Don't you feel it sometimes in 'Uncle Remus'?"

"True," said Paynter. "Perfectly true." And he looked at the lawyer with a new interest. The lawyer, who had been introduced as Mr. Ashe, was one of those people who are more worth looking at than most people realize when they look. If Napoleon had been red-haired, and had bent all his powers with a curious contentment upon the petty lawsuits of a province, he might have looked much the same; the head with the red hair was heavy and powerful; the figure in its dark, quiet clothes was comparatively insignificant, as was Napoleon's. He seemed more at ease in the Squire's society than the doctor, who, though a gentleman, was a shy one, and a mere shadow of his professional brother.

"As you truly say," remarked Paynter, "the story seems touched with quite barbarous elements, probably Negro. Originally, though, I think there was really a hagiological story about some hermit, though some of the higher critics say St. Securis never existed, but was only an allegory of arboriculture, since his name is the Latin for an ax."

"Oh, if you come to that," remarked the poet Treherne, "you might as well say Squire Vane doesn't exist, and that he's only an allegory for a weathercock." Something a shade too cool about this sally drew the lawyer's red brows together. He looked across the table and met the poet's somewhat equivocal smile.

"Do I understand, Mr. Treherne," asked Ashe, "that you support the miraculous claims of St. Securis in this case. Do you, by any chance, believe in the walking trees?"

"I see men as trees walking," answered the poet, "like the man cured of blindness in the Gospel. By the way, do I understand that you support the miraculous claims of that—thaumaturgist?"

Paynter intervened swiftly and suavely. "Now that sounds a fascinating piece of psychology. You see men as trees?"

"As I can't imagine why men should walk, I can't imagine why trees shouldn't," answered Treherne.

"Obviously, it is the nature of the organism", interposed the medical guest, Dr. Burton Brown; "it is necessary in the very type of vegetable structure."

"In other words, a tree sticks in the mud from year's end to year's end," answered Treherne. "So do you stop in your consulting room from ten to eleven every day. And don't you fancy a fairy, looking in at your window for a flash after having just jumped over the moon and played mulberry bush with the Pleiades, would think you were a vegetable structure, and that sitting still was the nature of the organism?"

"I don't happen to believe in fairies," said the doctor rather stiffly, for the argumentum ad hominem was becoming too common. A sulphurous subconscious anger seemed to radiate from the dark poet.

"Well, I should hope not, Doctor," began the Squire, in his loud and friendly style, and then stopped, seeing the other's attention arrested. The silent butler waiting on the guests had appeared behind the doctor's chair, and was saying something in the low, level tones of the well-trained servant. He was so smooth a specimen of the type that others never noticed, at first, that he also repeated the dark portrait, however varnished, so common in this particular family of Cornish Celts. His face was sallow and even yellow, and his hair indigo black. He went by the name of Miles. Some felt oppressed by the tribal type in this tiny corner of England. They felt somehow as if all these dark faces were the masks of a secret society.

The doctor rose with a half apology. "I must ask pardon for disturbing this pleasant party; I am called away on duty. Please don't let anybody move. We have to be ready for these things, you know. Perhaps Mr. Treherne will admit that my habits are not so very vegetable, after all." With this Parthian shaft, at which there was some laughter, he strode away very rapidly across the sunny lawn to where the road dipped down toward the village.

"He is very good among the poor," said the girl with an honorable seriousness.

"A capital fellow," agreed the Squire. "Where is Miles? You will have a cigar, Mr. Treherne?" And he got up from the table; the rest followed, and the group broke up on the lawn.

"Remarkable man, Treherne," said the American to the lawyer conversationally.

"Remarkable is the word," assented Ashe rather grimly. "But I don't think I'll make any remark about him."

The Squire, too impatient to wait for the yellow-faced Miles, had betaken himself indoors for the cigars, and Barbara found herself once more paired off with the poet, as she floated along the terrace garden; but this time, symbolically enough, upon the same level of lawn. Mr. Treherne looked less eccentric after having shed his curious cloak, and seemed a quieter and more casual figure.

"I didn't mean to be rude to you just now," she said abruptly.

"And that's the worst of it," replied the man of letters, "for I'm horribly afraid I did mean to be rude to you. When I looked up and saw you up there something surged up in me that was in all the revolutions of history. Oh, there was admiration in it too! Perhaps there was idolatry in all the iconoclasts."

He seemed to have a power of reaching rather intimate conversation in one silent and cat-like bound, as he had scaled the steep road, and it made her feel him to be dangerous, and perhaps unscrupulous. She changed the subject sharply, not without it movement toward gratifying her own curiosity.

"What *did* you mean by all that about walking trees?" she asked. "Don't tell me you really believe in a magic tree that eats birds!"

"I should probably surprise you," said Treherne gravely, "more by what I don't believe than by what I do."

Then, after a pause, he made a general gesture toward the house and garden. "I'm afraid I don't believe in all this; for instance, in Elizabethan houses and Elizabethan families and the way estates have been improved, and the rest of it. Look at our friend the woodcutter now." And he pointed to the man with the quaint black beard, who was still plying his ax upon the timber below.

"That man's family goes back for ages, and it was far richer and freer in what you call the Dark Ages than it is now. Wait till the Cornish peasant writes a history of Cornwall."

"But what in the world," she demanded, "has this to do with whether you believe in a tree eating birds?"

"Why should I confess what I believe in?" he said, a muffled drum of mutiny in his voice. "The gentry came here and took our land and took our labor and took our customs. And now, after exploitation, a viler thing, education! They must take our dreams!"

"Well, this dream was rather a nightmare, wasn't it?" asked Barbara, smiling; and the next moment grew quite grave, saying almost anxiously: "But here's Doctor Brown back again. Why, he looks quite upset."

The doctor, a black figure on the green lawn, was, indeed, coming toward them at a very vigorous walk. His body and gait very much younger than his face, which seemed prematurely lined as with worry; his brow was bald, and projected from the straight, dark hair behind it. He was visibly paler than when he left the lunch table.

"I am sorry to say, Miss Vane," he said, "that I am the bearer of bad news to poor Martin, the woodman here. His daughter died half an hour ago."

"Oh," cried Barbara warmly, "I am *so* sorry!"

"So am I," said the doctor, and passed on rather abruptly; he ran down the stone steps between the stone urns; and they saw him in talk with the woodcutter. They could not see the woodcutter's face. He stood with his back to them, but they saw something that seemed more moving than any change of countenance. The man's hand holding the ax rose high above his head, and for a flash it seemed as if he would have cut down the doctor. But in fact he was not looking at the doctor. His face was set toward the cliff, where, sheer out of the dwarf forest, rose, gigantic and gilded by the sun, the trees of pride.

The strong brown hand made a movement and was empty. The ax went circling swiftly through the air, its head showing like a silver crescent against the gray twilight of the trees. It did not reach its tall objective, but fell among the undergrowth, shaking up a flying litter of birds. But in the poet's memory, full of primal things, something seemed to say that he had seen the birds of some pagan augury, the ax of some pagan sacrifice.

A moment after the man made a heavy movement forward, as if to recover his tool; but the doctor put a hand on his arm.

"Never mind that now," they heard him say sadly and kindly. "The Squire will excuse you any more work, I know."

Something made the girl look at Treherne. He stood gazing, his head a little bent, and one of his black elf-locks had fallen forward over his forehead. And again she had the sense of a shadow over the grass; she almost felt as if the grass were a host of fairies, and that the fairies were not her friends.

II. THE WAGER OF SQUIRE VANE

IT was more than a month before the legend of the peacock trees was again discussed in the Squire's circle. It fell out one evening, when his eccentric taste for meals in the garden that gathered the company round the same table, now lit with a lamp and laid out for dinner in a glowing spring twilight. It was even the same company, for in the few weeks intervening they had insensibly grown more and more into each other's lives, forming a little group like a club. The American aesthete was of course the most active agent, his resolution to pluck out the heart of the Cornish poet's mystery leading him again and again to influence his flighty host for such reunions. Even Mr. Ashe, the lawyer, seemed to have swallowed his half-humorous prejudices; and the doctor, though a rather sad and silent, was a companionable and considerate man. Paynter had even read Treherne's poetry aloud, and he read admirably; he had also read other things, not aloud, grubbing up everything in the neighborhood, from guidebooks to epitaphs, that could throw a light on local antiquities. And it was that evening when the lamplight and the last daylight had kindled the colors of the wine and silver on the table under the tree, that he announced a new discovery.

"Say, Squire," he remarked, with one of his rare Americanisms, "about those bogey trees of yours; I don't believe you know half the tales told round here about them. It seems they have a way of eating things. Not that I have any ethical objection to eating things," he continued, helping himself elegantly to green cheese. "But I have more or less, broadly speaking, an objection to eating people."

"Eating people!" repeated Barbara Vane.

"I know a globe-trotter mustn't be fastidious," replied Mr. Paynter. "But I repeat firmly, an objection to eating people. The peacock trees seem to have progressed since the happy days of innocence when they only ate peacocks. If you ask the people here—the fisherman who lives on that beach, or the man that mows this very lawn in front of us—they'll tell you tales taller than any tropical one I brought you from the Barbary Coast. If you ask them what happened to the fisherman Peters, who got drunk on All Hallows Eve, they'll tell you he lost his way in that little wood, tumbled down asleep under the wicked trees, and then—evaporated, vanished, was licked up like dew by the sun. If you ask them where Harry Hawke is, the widow's little son, they'll just tell you he's swallowed; that he was dared to climb the trees and sit there all night, and did it. What the trees did God knows; the habits of a vegetable ogre leave one a little vague. But they even add the agreeable detail that a new branch appears on the tree when somebody has petered out in this style."

"What new nonsense is this?" cried Vane. "I know there's some crazy yarn about the trees spreading fever, though every educated man knows why these epidemics return occasionally. And I know they say you can tell the noise of them among other trees in a gale, and I dare say you can. But even Cornwall isn't a lunatic asylum, and a tree that dines on a passing tourist—"

"Well, the two tales are reconcilable enough," put in the poet quietly. "If there were a magic that killed men when they came close, it's likely to strike them with sickness when they stand far off. In the old romance the dragon, that devours people, often blasts others with a sort of poisonous breath."

Ashe looked across at the speaker steadily, not to say stonily.

"Do I understand," he inquired, "that you swallow the swallowing trees too?"

Treherne's dark smile was still on the defensive; his fencing always annoyed the other, and he seemed not without malice in the matter.

"Swallowing is a metaphor," he said, "about me, if not about the trees. And metaphors take us at once into dreamland—no bad place, either. This garden, I think, gets more and more like a dream at this corner of the day and night, that might lead us anywhere."

The yellow horn of the moon had appeared silently and as if suddenly over the black horns of the seaweed, seeming to announce as night something which till then had been evening. A night breeze came in between the trees and raced stealthily across the turf, and as they ceased speaking they heard, not only the seething grass, but the sea itself move and sound in all the cracks and caves round them and below them and on every side. They all felt the note that had been struck—the American as an art critic and the poet as a poet; and the Squire, who believed himself boiling with an impatience purely rational, did not really understand his own impatience. In him, more perhaps than the others—more certainly than he knew himself—the sea wind went to the head like wine.

"Credulity is a curious thing," went on Treherne in a low voice. "It is more negative than positive, and yet it is infinite. Hundreds of men will avoid walking under a ladder; they don't know where the door of the ladder will lead. They don't really think God would throw a thunderbolt at them for such a thing. They don't know what would happen, that is just the point; but yet they step aside as from a precipice. So the poor people here may or may not believe anything; they don't go into those trees at night."

"I walk under a ladder whenever I can," cried Vane, in quite unnecessary excitement.

"You belong to a Thirteen Club," said the poet. "You walk under a ladder on Friday to dine thirteen at a table, everybody spilling the salt. But even you don't go into those trees at night."

Squire Vane stood up, his silver hair flaming in the wind.

"I'll stop all night in your tomfool wood and up your tomfool trees," he said. "I'll do it for twopence or two thousand pounds, if anyone will take the bet."

Without waiting for reply, he snatched up his wide white hat and settled it on with a fierce gesture, and had gone off in great leonine strides across the lawn before anyone at the table could move.

The stillness was broken by Miles, the butler, who dropped and broke one of the plates he carried. He stood looking after his master with his long, angular chin thrust out, looking yellower where it caught the yellow light of the lamp below. His face was thus sharply in shadow, but Paynter fancied for a moment it was convulsed by some passion passing surprise. But the face was quite as usual when it turned, and Paynter realized that a night of fancies had begun, like the cross purposes of the "Midsummer Night's Dream."

The wood of the strange trees, toward which the Squire was walking, lay so far forward on the headland, which ultimately almost overhung the sea, that it could be approached by only one path, which shone clearly like a silver ribbon in the twilight. The ribbon ran along the edge of the cliff, where the single row of deformed trees ran beside it all the way, and eventually plunged into the closer mass of trees by one natural gateway, a mere gap in the wood, looking dark, like a lion's mouth. What became of the path inside could not be seen, but it doubtless led round the hidden roots of the great central trees. The Squire was already within a yard or two of this dark entry when his daughter rose from the table and took a step or two after him as if to call him back.

Treherne had also risen, and stood as if dazed at the effect of his idle defiance. When Barbara moved he seemed to recover himself, and stepping after her, said something which Paynter did not hear. He said it casually and even distantly enough, but it clearly suggested something to her mind; for, after a moment's thought, she nodded and walked back, not toward the table, but apparently toward the house. Paynter looked after her with a momentary curiosity, and when he turned again the Squire had vanished into the hole in the wood.

"He's gone," said Treherne, with a clang of finality in his tones, like the slamming of a door.

"Well, suppose he has?" cried the lawyer, roused at the voice. "The Squire can go into his own wood, I suppose! What the devil's all the fuss about, Mr. Paynter? Don't tell me you think there's any harm in that plantation of sticks."

"No, I don't," said Paynter, throwing one leg over another and lighting a cigar. "But I shall stop here till he comes out."

"Very well," said Ashe shortly, "I'll stop with you, if only to see the end of this farce."

The doctor said nothing, but he also kept his seat and accepted one of the American's cigars. If Treherne had been attending to the matter he might have noted, with his sardonic superstition, a curious fact—that, while all three men were tacitly condemning themselves to stay out all night if necessary, all, by one blank omission or oblivion, assumed that it was impossible to follow their host into the wood just in front of them. But Treherne, though still in the garden, had wandered away from the garden table, and was pacing along the single line of trees against the dark sea. They had in their regular interstices, showing the sea as through a series of windows, something of the look of the ghost or skeleton of a cloister, and he, having thrown his coat once more over his neck, like a cape, passed to and fro like the ghost of some not very sane monk.

All these men, whether skeptics or mystics, looked back for the rest of their lives on that night as on something unnatural. They sat still or started up abruptly, and paced the great garden in long detours, so that it seemed that no three of them were together at a time, and none knew who would be his companion; yet their rambling remained within the same dim and mazy space. They fell into snatches of uneasy slumber; these were very brief, and yet they felt as if the whole sitting, strolling, or occasional speaking had been parts of a single dream.

Paynter woke once, and found Ashe sitting opposite him at a table otherwise empty; his face dark in shadow and his cigar-end like the red eye of a Cyclops. Until the lawyer spoke, in his steady voice, Paynter was positively afraid of him. He answered at random and nodded again; when he again woke the lawyer was gone, and what was opposite him was the bald, pale brow of the doctor; there seemed suddenly something ominous in the familiar fact that he wore spectacles. And yet the vanishing Ashe had only vanished a few yards away, for he turned at that instant and strolled back to the table. With a jerk Paynter realized that his nightmare was but a trick of sleep or sleeplessness, and spoke in his natural voice, but rather loud.

"So you've joined us again; where's Treherne?"

"Oh, still revolving, I suppose, like a polar bear under those trees on the cliff," replied Ashe, motioning with his cigar, "looking at what an older (and you will forgive me for thinking a somewhat better) poet called the wine-dark sea. It really has a sort of purple shade; look at it."

Paynter looked; he saw the wine-dark sea and the fantastic trees that fringed it, but he did not see the poet; the cloister was already empty of its restless monk.

"Gone somewhere else," he said, with futility far from characteristic. "He'll be back here presently. This is an interesting vigil, but a vigil loses some of its intensity when you can't keep awake. Ah! Here's Treherne; so we're all mustered, as the politician said when Mr. Colman came late for dinner. No, the doctor's off again. How restless we all are!" The poet had drawn near, his feet were falling soft on the grass, and was gazing at them with a singular attentiveness.

"It will soon be over," he said.

"What?" snapped Ashe very abruptly.

"The night, of course," replied Treherne in a motionless manner. "The darkest hour has passed."

"Didn't some other minor poet remark," inquired Paynter flippantly, "that the darkest hour before the dawn—? My God, what was that? It was like a scream."

"It was a scream," replied the poet. "The scream of a peacock."

Ashe stood up, his strong pale face against his red hair, and said furiously: "What the devil do you mean?"

"Oh, perfectly natural causes, as Dr. Brown would say," replied Treherne. "Didn't the Squire tell us the trees had a shrill note of their own when the wind blew? The wind's beating up again from the sea; I shouldn't wonder if there was a storm before dawn."

Dawn indeed came gradually with a growing noise of wind, and the purple sea began to boil about the dark volcanic cliffs. The first change in the sky showed itself only in the shapes of the wood and the single stems growing darker but clearer; and above the gray clump, against a glimpse of growing light, they saw aloft the evil trinity of the trees. In their long lines there seemed to Paynter something faintly serpentine and even spiral. He could almost fancy he saw them slowly revolving as in some cyclic dance, but this, again, was but a last delusion of dreamland, for a few seconds later he was again asleep. In dreams he toiled through a tangle of inconclusive tales, each filled with the same stress and noise of sea and sea wind; and above and outside all other voices the wailing of the Trees of Pride.

When he woke it was broad day, and a bloom of early light lay on wood and garden and on fields and farms for miles away. The comparative common sense that daylight brings even to the sleepless drew him alertly to his feet, and showed him all his companions standing about the lawn in similar attitudes of expectancy. There was no need to ask what they were expecting. They were waiting to hear the nocturnal experiences, comic or commonplace or whatever they might prove to be, of that eccentric friend, whose experiment (whether from some subconscious fear or some fancy of honor) they had not ventured to interrupt. Hour followed hour, and still nothing stirred in the wood save an occasional bird. The Squire, like most men of his type, was an early riser, and it was not likely that he would in this case sleep late; it was much more likely, in the excitement in which he had left them, that he would not sleep at all. Yet it was clear that he must be sleeping, perhaps by some reaction from a strain. By the time the sun was high in heaven Ashe the lawyer, turning to the others, spoke abruptly and to the point.

"Shall we go into the wood now?" asked Paynter, and almost seemed to hesitate.

"I will go in," said Treherne simply. Then, drawing up his dark head in answer to their glances, he added:

"No, do not trouble yourselves. It is never the believer who is afraid."

For the second time they saw a man mount the white curling path and disappear into the gray tangled wood, but this time they did not have to wait long to see him again.

A few minutes later he reappeared in the woodland gateway, and came slowly toward them across the grass. He stopped before the doctor, who stood nearest, and said something. It was repeated to the others, and went round the ring with low cries of incredulity. The others plunged into the wood and returned wildly, and were seen speaking to others again who gathered from the house; the wild wireless telegraphy which is the education of countryside communities spread it farther and farther before the fact itself was fully realized; and before nightfall a quarter of the county knew that Squire Vane had vanished like a burst bubble.

Widely as the wild story was repeated, and patiently as it was pondered, it was long before there was even the beginning of a sequel to it. In the interval Paynter had politely removed himself from the house of mourning, or rather of questioning, but only so far as the village inn; for Barbara Vane was glad of the traveler's experience and sympathy, in addition to that afforded her by the lawyer and doctor as old friends of the family. Even Treherne was not discouraged from his occasional visits with a view to helping the hunt for the lost man. The five held many counsels round the old garden table, at which the unhappy master of the house had dined for the last time; and Barbara wore her old mask of stone, if it was now a more tragic mask. She had shown no passion after the first morning of discovery, when she had broken forth once, speaking strangely enough in the view of some of her hearers.

She had come slowly out of the house, to which her own or some one else's wisdom had relegated her during the night of the wager; and it was clear from her face that somebody had told her the truth; Miles, the butler, stood on the steps behind her; and it was probably he.

"Do not be much distressed, Miss Vane," said Doctor Brown, in a low and rather uncertain voice. "The search in the wood has hardly begun. I am convinced we shall find—something quite simple."

"The doctor is right," said Ashe, in his firm tones; "I myself—"

"The doctor is not right," said the girl, turning a white face on the speaker, "I know better. The poet is right. The poet is always right. Oh, he has been here from the beginning of the world, and seen wonders and terrors that are all round our path, and only hiding behind a bush or a stone. You and your doctoring and your science—why, you have only been here for a few fumbling generations; and you can't conquer even your own enemies of the flesh. Oh, forgive me, Doctor, I know you do splendidly; but the fever comes in the village, and the people die and die for all that. And now it's my poor father. God help us all! The only thing left is to believe in God; for we can't help believing in devils." And she left them, still walking quite slowly, but in such a fashion that no one could go after her.

The spring had already begun to ripen into summer, and spread a green tent from the tree over the garden table, when the American visitor, sitting there with his two professional companions, broke the silence by saying what had long been in his mind.

"Well," he said, "I suppose whatever we may think it wise to say, we have all begun to think of a possible conclusion. It can't be put very delicately anyhow; but, after all, there's a very necessary business side to it. What are we going to do about poor Vane's affairs, apart from himself? I suppose you know," he added, in a low voice to the lawyer, "whether he made a will?"

"He left everything to his daughter unconditionally," replied Ashe. "But nothing can be done with it. There's no proof whatever that he's dead." "No legal proof?" remarked Paynter dryly. A wrinkle of irritation had appeared in the big bald brow of Doctor Brown; and he made an impatient movement.

"Of course he's dead," he said. "What's the sense of all this legal fuss? We were watching this side of the wood, weren't we? A man couldn't have flown off those high cliffs over the sea; he could only have fallen off. What else can he be but dead?"

"I speak as a lawyer," returned Ashe, raising his eyebrows. "We can't presume his death, or have an inquest or anything till we find the poor fellow's body, or some remains that may reasonably be presumed to be his body."

"I see," observed Paynter quietly. "You speak as a lawyer; but I don't think it's very hard to guess what you think as a man."

"I own I'd rather be a man than a lawyer," said the doctor, rather roughly. "I'd no notion the law was such an ass. What's the good of keeping the poor girl out of her property, and the estate all going to pieces? Well, I must be off, or my patients will be going to pieces too."

And with a curt salutation he pursued his path down to the village.

"That man does his duty, if anybody does," remarked Paynter. "We must pardon his—shall I say manners or manner?"

"Oh, I bear him no malice," replied Ashe good-humoredly, "But I'm glad he's gone, because—well, because I don't want him to know how jolly right he is." And he leaned back in his chair and stared up at the roof of green leaves.

"You are sure," said Paynter, looking at the table, "that Squire Vane is dead?"

"More than that," said Ashe, still staring at the leaves. "I'm sure of how he died."

"Ah!" said the American, with an intake of breath, and they remained for a moment, one gazing at the tree and the other at the table.

"Sure is perhaps too strong a word," continued Ashe. "But my conviction will want some shaking. I don't envy the counsel for the defense."

"The counsel for the defense," repeated Paynter, and looked up quickly at his companion. He was struck again by the man's Napoleonic chin and jaw, as he had been when they first talked of the legend of St. Securis.

"Then," he began, "you don't think the trees—"

"The trees be damned!" snorted the lawyer. "The tree had two legs on that evening. What our friend the poet," he added, with a sneer, "would call a walking tree. Apropos of our friend the poet, you seemed surprised that night to find he was not walking poetically by the sea all the time, and I fear I affected to share your ignorance. I was not so sure then as I am now."

"Sure of what?" demanded the other.

"To begin with," said Ashe, "I'm sure our friend the poet followed Vane into the wood that night, for I saw him coming out again."

Paynter leaned forward, suddenly pale with excitement, and struck the wooden table so that it rattled.

"Mr. Ashe, you're wrong," he cried. "You're a wonderful man and you're wrong. You've probably got tons of true convincing evidence, and you're wrong. I know this poet; I know him as a poet; and that's just what you don't. I know you think he gave you crooked answers, and seemed to be all smiles and black looks at once; but you don't understand the type. I know now why you don't understand the Irish. Sometimes you think it's soft, and sometimes sly, and sometimes murderous, and sometimes uncivilized; and all the time it's only civilized; quivering with the sensitive irony of understanding all that you don't understand."

"Well," said Ashe shortly, "we'll see who's right."

"We will," cried Cyprian, and rose suddenly from the table. All the drooping of the aesthete had dropped from him; his Yankee accent rose high, like a horn of defiance, and there was nothing about him but the New World.

"I guess I will look into this myself," he said, stretching his long limbs like an athlete. "I search that little wood of yours to-morrow. It's a bit late, or I'd do it now."

"The wood has been searched," said the lawyer, rising also.

"Yes," drawled the American. "It's been searched by servants, policemen, local policeman, and quite a lot of people; and do you know I have a notion that nobody round here is likely to have searched it at all."

"And what are you going to do with it?" asked Ashe.

"What I bet they haven't done," replied Cyprian. "I'm going to climb a tree."

And with a quaint air of renewed cheerfulness he took himself away at a rapid walk to his inn.

He appeared at daybreak next morning outside the Vane Arms with all the air of one setting out on his travels in distant lands. He had a field glass slung over his shoulder, and a very large sheath knife buckled by a belt round his waist, and carried with the cool bravado of the bowie knife of a

cowboy. But in spite of this backwoodsman's sim-
plicity, or perhaps rather because of it, he eyed with
rising relish the picturesque plan and sky line of
the antiquated village, and especially the wooden
square of the old inn sign that hung over his head; a
shield, of which the charges seemed to him a mere
medley of blue dolphins, gold crosses, and scarlet
birds. The colors and cubic corners of that painted
board pleased him like a play or a puppet show. He
stood staring and straddling for some moments on
the cobbles of the little market place; then he gave
a short laugh and began to mount the steep streets
toward the high park and garden beyond. From the
high lawn, above the tree and table, he could see on
one side the land stretch away past the house into
a great rolling plain, which under the clear edges of
the dawn seemed dotted with picturesque details.
The woods here and there on the plain looked like
green hedgehogs, as grotesque as the incongruous
beasts found unaccountably walking in the blank
spaces of mediaeval maps. The land, cut up into colored fields, recalled the heraldry of the signboard;
this also was at once ancient and gay. On the other
side the ground to seaward swept down and then up
again to the famous or infamous wood; the square
of strange trees lay silently tilted on the slope, also
suggesting, if not a map, or least a bird's-eye view.
Only the triple centerpiece of the peacock trees rose
clear of the sky line; and these stood up in tranquil
sunlight as things almost classical, a triangular
temple of the winds. They seemed pagan in a newer and more placid sense; and he felt a newer and
more boyish curiosity and courage for the consulting of the oracle. In all his wanderings he had never
walked so lightly, for the connoisseur of sensations

had found something to do at last; he was fighting for a friend.

He was brought to a standstill once, however, and that at the very gateway of the garden of the trees of knowledge. Just outside the black entry of the wood, now curtained with greener and larger leafage, he came on a solitary figure.

It was Martin, the woodcutter, wading in the bracken and looking about him in rather a lost fashion. The man seemed to be talking to himself.

"I dropped it here," he was saying. "But I'll never work with it again I reckon. Doctor wouldn't let me pick it up, when I wanted to pick it up; and now they've got it, like they've got the Squire. Wood and iron, wood and iron, but eating it's nothing to them."

"Come!" said Paynter kindly, remembering the man's domestic trouble. "Miss Vane will see you have anything you want, I know. And look here, don't brood on all those stories about the Squire. Is there the slightest trace of the trees having anything to do with it? Is there even this extra branch the idiots talked about?"

There had been growing on Paynter the suspicion that the man before him was not perfectly sane; yet he was much more startled by the sudden and cold sanity that looked for an instant out of the woodman's eyes, as he answered in his ordinary manner.

"Well, sir, did you count the branches before?"

Then he seemed to relapse; and Paynter left him wandering and wavering in the undergrowth; and entered the wood like one across whose sunny path a shadow has fallen for an instant.

Diving under the wood, he was soon threading a leafy path which, even under that summer sun, shone only with an emerald twilight, as if it were on the floor of the sea. It wound about more shakily than he had supposed, as if resolved to approach the central trees as if they were the heart of the maze at Hampton Court. They were the heart of the maze for him, anyhow; he sought them as straight as a crooked road would carry him; and, turning a final corner, he beheld, for the first time, the foundations of those towers of vegetation he had as yet only seen from above, as they stood waist-high in the woodland. He found the suspicion correct which supposed the tree branched from one great root, like a candelabrum; the fork, though stained and slimy with green fungoids, was quite near the ground, and offered a first foothold. He put his foot in it, and without a flash of hesitation went aloft, like Jack climbing the Bean stalk.

Above him the green roof of leaves and boughs seemed sealed like a firmament of foliage; but, by bending and breaking the branches to right and left he slowly forced a passage upward; and had at last, and suddenly, the sensation coming out on the top of the world. He felt as if he had never been in the open air before. Sea and land lay in a circle below and about him, as he sat astride a branch of the tall tree; he was almost surprised to see the sun still comparatively low in the sky; as if he were looking over a land of eternal sunrise.

"Silent upon a peak in Darien," he remarked, in a needlessly loud and cheerful voice; and though the claim, thus expressed, was illogical, it was not inappropriate. He did feel as if he were a primitive adventurer just come to the New World, instead of a modern traveler just come from it.

"I wonder," he proceeded, "whether I am really the first that ever burst into this silent tree. It looks like it. Those—"

He stopped and sat on his branch quite motionless, but his eyes were turned on a branch a little below it, and they were brilliant with a vigilance, like those of a man watching a snake.

What he was looking at might, at first sight, have been a large white fungus spreading on the smooth and monstrous trunk; but it was not.

Leaning down dangerously from his perch, he detached it from the twig on which it had caught, and then sat holding it in his hand and gazing at it. It was Squire Vane's white Panama hat, but there was no Squire Vane under it. Paynter felt a nameless relief in the very fact that there was not.

There in the clear sunlight and sea air, for an instant, all the tropical terrors of his own idle tale surrounded and suffocated him. It seemed indeed some demon tree of the swamps; a vegetable serpent that fed on men. Even the hideous farce in the fancy of digesting a whole man with the exception of his hat, seemed only to simplify the nightmare. And he found himself gazing dully at one leaf of the tree, which happened to be turned toward him, so that the odd markings, which had partly made the legend, really looked a little like the eye in a peacock's feather. It was as if the sleeping tree had opened one eye upon him.

With a sharp effort he steadied himself in mind and posture on the bough; his reason returned, and he began to descend with the hat in his teeth. When he was back in the underworld of the wood, he studied the hat again and with closer attention. In one place in the crown there was a hole or rent, which certainly had not been there when it had last lain on the table under the garden tree. He sat down, lit a cigarette, and reflected for a long time.

A wood, even a small wood, is not an easy thing to search minutely; but he provided himself with some practical tests in the matter. In one sense the very density of the thicket was a help; he could at least see where anyone had strayed from the path, by broken and trampled growths of every kind. After many hours' industry, he had made a sort of new map of the place; and had decided beyond doubt that some person or persons had so strayed, for some purpose, in several defined directions. There was a way burst through the bushes, making a short cut across a loop of the wandering path; there was another forking out from it as an alternative way into the central space. But there was one especially which was unique, and which seemed to him, the more he studied it, to point to some essential of the mystery.

One of these beaten and broken tracks went from the space under the peacock trees outward into the wood for about twenty yards and then stopped. Beyond that point not a twig was broken nor a leaf disturbed. It had no exit, but he could not believe that it had no goal. After some further reflection, he knelt down and began to cut away grass and clay with his knife, and was surprised at the ease with which they detached themselves. In a few moments a whole section of the soil lifted like a lid; it was a round lid and presented a quaint appearance, like a flat cap with green feathers. For though the disc itself was made of wood, there was a layer of earth on it with the live grass still growing there. And the removal of the round lid revealed a round hole, black as night and seemingly bottomless. Paynter understood it instantly. It was rather near the sea for a well to be sunk, but the traveler had known wells sunk even nearer. He rose to his feet with the great knife in his hand, a frown on his face, and his doubts resolved. He no longer shrank from naming what he knew. This was not the first corpse that had been thrown down a well; here, without stone or epitaph, was the grave of Squire Vane. In a flash all the mythological follies about saints and peacocks were forgotten; he was knocked on the head, as with a stone club, by the human common sense of crime.

Cyprian Paynter stood long by the well in the wood, walked round it in meditation, examined its rim and the ring of grass about it, searched the surrounding soil thoroughly, came back and stood beside the well once more. His researches and reflections had been so long that he had not realized that the day had passed and that the wood and the world round it were beginning already to be steeped in the enrichment of evening. The day had been radiantly calm; the sea seemed to be as still as the well, and the well was as still as a mirror. And then, quite without warning, the mirror moved of itself like a living thing.

In the well, in the wood, the water leapt and gurgled, with a grotesque noise like something swallowing, and then settled again with a second sound. Cyprian could not see into the well clearly, for the opening, from where he stood, was an ellipse, a mere slit, and half masked by thistles and rank grass like a green beard. For where he stood now was three yards away from the well, and he had not yet himself realized that he had sprung back all that distance from the brink when the water spoke.

III. THE MYSTERY OF THE WELL

Cyprian Paynter did not know what he expected to see rise out of the well—the corpse of the murdered man or merely the spirit of the fountain. Anyhow, neither of them rose out of it, and he recognized after an instant that this was, after all, perhaps the more natural course of things. Once more he pulled himself together, walked to the edge of the well and looked down. He saw, as before, a dim glimmer of water, at that depth no brighter than ink; he fancied he still heard a faint convulsion and murmur, but it gradually subsided to an utter stillness. Short of suicidally diving in, there was nothing to be done. He realized that, with all his equipment, he had not even brought anything like a rope or basket, and at length decided to return for them. As he retraced his steps to the entrance, he recurred to, and took stock of, his more solid discoveries. Somebody had gone into the wood, killed the Squire and thrown him down the well, but he did not admit for a moment that it was his friend the poet; but if the latter had actually been seen coming out of the wood the matter was serious. As he walked the rapidly darkening twilight was cloven with red gleams, that made him almost fancy for a moment that some fantastic criminal had set fire to the tiny forest as he fled. A second glance showed him nothing but one of those red sunsets in which such serene days sometimes close.

As he came out of the gloomy gate of trees into the full glow he saw a dark figure standing quite still in the dim bracken, on the spot where he had left the woodcutter. It was not the woodcutter.

It was topped by a tall black hat of a funeral type, and the whole figure stood so black against the field of crimson fire that edged the sky line that he could not for an instant understand or recall it. When he did, it was with an odd change in the whole channel of his thoughts.

"Doctor Brown!" he cried. "Why, what are you doing up here?"

"I have been talking to poor Martin," answered the doctor, and made a rather awkward movement with his hand toward the road down to the village. Following the gesture, Paynter dimly saw another dark figure walking down in the blood-red distance. He also saw that the hand motioning was really black, and not merely in shadow; and, coming nearer, found the doctor's dress was really funereal, down to the detail of the dark gloves. It gave the American a small but queer shock, as if this were actually an undertaker come up to bury the corpse that could not be found.

"Poor Martin's been looking for his chopper," observed Doctor Brown, "but I told him I'd picked it
up and kept it for him. Between ourselves, I hardly
think he's fit to be trusted with it." Then, seeing
the glance at his black garb, he added: "I've just
been to a funeral. Did you know there's been another loss? Poor Jake the fisherman's wife, down
in the cottage on the shore, you know. This infernal fever, of course."

As they both turned, facing the red evening light,
Paynter instinctively made a closer study, not merely of the doctor's clothes, but of the doctor. Dr. Burton Brown was a tall, alert man, neatly dressed,
who would otherwise have had an almost military
air but for his spectacles and an almost painful in-
tellectualism in his lean brown face and bald brow.
The contrast was clinched by the fact that, while his
face was of the ascetic type generally conceived as
clean-shaven, he had a strip of dark mustache cut
too short for him to bite, and yet a mouth that often
moved as if trying to bite it. He might have been
a very intelligent army surgeon, but he had more
the look of an engineer or one of those services that
combine a military silence with a more than military science. Paynter had always respected something ruggedly reliable about the man, and after a
little hesitation he told him all the discoveries.

The doctor took the hat of the dead Squire in his
hand, and examined it with frowning care. He put
one finger through the hole in the crown and moved
it meditatively. And Paynter realized how fanciful
his own fatigue must have made him; for so silly a
thing as the black finger waggling through the rent

in that frayed white relic unreasonably displeased him. The doctor soon made the same discovery with professional acuteness, and applied it much further. For when Paynter began to tell him of the moving water in the well he looked at him a moment through his spectacles, and then said:

"Did you have any lunch?"

Paynter for the first time realized that he had, as a fact, worked and thought furiously all day without food.

"Please don't fancy I mean you had too much lunch," said the medical man, with mournful humor. "On the contrary, I mean you had too little. I think you are a bit knocked out, and your nerves exaggerate things. Anyhow, let me advise you not to do any more to-night. There's nothing to be done without ropes or some sort of fishing tackle, if with that; but I think I can get you some of the sort of grappling irons the fishermen use for dragging. Poor Jake's got some, I know; I'll bring them round to you to-morrow morning. The fact is, I'm staying there for a bit as he's rather in a state, and I think is better for me to ask for the things and not a stranger. I am sure you'll understand."

Paynter understood sufficiently to assent, and hardly knew why he stood vacantly watching the doctor make his way down the steep road to the shore and the fisher's cottage. Then he threw off thoughts he had not examined, or even consciously entertained, and walked slowly and rather heavily back to the Vane Arms.

The doctor, still funereal in manner, though no longer so in costume, appeared punctually under the wooden sign next morning, laden with what he had promised; an apparatus of hooks and a hanging net for hoisting up anything sunk to a reasonable depth. He was about to proceed on his professional round, and said nothing further to deter the American from proceeding on his own very unprofessional experiment as a detective. That buoyant amateur had indeed recovered most, if not all, of yesterday's buoyancy, was now well fitted to pass any medical examination, and returned with all his own energy to the scene of yesterday's labors.

It may well have brightened and made breezier his second day's toil that he had not only the sunlight and the bird's singing in the little wood, to say nothing of a more scientific apparatus to work with, but also human companionship, and that of the most intelligent type. After leaving the doctor and before leaving the village he had bethought himself of seeking the little court or square where stood the quiet brown house of Andrew Ashe, solicitor, and the operations of dragging were worked in double harness. Two heads were peering over the well in the wood: one yellow-haired, lean and eager; the other redhaired, heavy and pondering; and if it be true that two heads are better than one, it is truer that four hands are better than two. In any case, their united and repeated efforts bore fruit at last, if anything so hard and meager and forlorn can be called a fruit. It weighed loosely in the net as it was lifted, and rolled out on the grassy edge of the well; it was a bone.

Ashe picked it up and stood with it in his hand, frowning.

"We want Doctor Brown here," he said. "This may be the bone of some animal. Any dog or sheep might fall into a hidden well." Then he broke off, for his companion was already detaching a second bone from the net.

After another half hour's effort Paynter had occasion to remark, "It must have been rather a large dog." There were already a heap of such white fragments at his feet.

"I have seen nothing yet," said Ashe, speaking more plainly. "That is certainly a human bone." "I fancy this must be a human bone," said the American.

And he turned away a little as he handed the other a skull.

There was no doubt of what sort of skull; there was the one unique curve that holds the mystery of reason, and underneath it the two black holes that had held human eyes. But just above that on the left was another and smaller black hole, which was not an eye.

Then the lawyer said, with something like an effort: "We may admit it is a man without admitting it is— any particular man. There may be something, after all, in that yarn about the drunkard; he may have tumbled into the well. Under certain conditions, after certain natural processes, I fancy, the bones might be stripped in this way, even without the skill of any assassin. We want the doctor again."

Then he added suddenly, and the very sound of his voice suggested that he hardly believed his own words.

"Haven't you got poor Vane's hat there?"

He took it from the silent American's hand, and with a sort of hurry fitted it on the bony head.

"Don't!" said the other involuntarily.

The lawyer had put his finger, as the doctor had done, through the hole in the hat, and it lay exactly over the hole in the skull.

"I have the better right to shrink," he said steadily, but in a vibrant voice. "I think I am the older friend."

Paynter nodded without speech, accepting the final identification. The last doubt, or hope, had departed, and he turned to the dragging apparatus, and did not speak till he had made his last find.

The singing of the birds seemed to grow louder about them, and the dance of the green summer leaves was repeated beyond in the dance of the green summer sea. Only the great roots of the mysterious trees could be seen, the rest being far aloft, and all round it was a wood of little, lively and happy things. They might have been two innocent naturalists, or even two children fishing for eels or tittlebats on that summer holiday when Paynter pulled up something that weighed in the net more heavily than any bone. It nearly broke the meshes, and fell against a mossy stone with a clang.

"Truth lies at the bottom of a well," cried the American, with lift in his voice. "The woodman's ax."

It lay, indeed, flat and gleaming in the grasses by the well in the wood, just as it had lain in the thicket where the woodman threw it in the beginning of all these things. But on one corner of the bright blade was a dull brown stain.

"I see," said Ashe, "the woodman's ax, and therefore the Woodman. Your deductions are rapid."

"My deductions are reasonable," said Paynter, "Look here, Mr. Ashe; I know what you're thinking. I know you distrust Treherne; but I'm sure you will be just for all that. To begin with, surely the first assumption is that the woodman's ax is used by the Woodman. What have you to say to it?"

"I say 'No' to it," replied the lawyer. "The last weapon a woodman would use would be a woodman's ax; that is if he is a sane man."

"He isn't," said Paynter quietly; "you said you wanted the doctor's opinion just now. The doctor's opinion on this point is the same as my own. We both found him meandering about outside there; it's obvious this business has gone to his head, at any rate. If the murderer were a man of business like yourself, what you say might be sound. But this murderer is a mystic. He was driven by some fanatical fad about the trees. It's quite likely he thought there was something solemn and sacrificial about the ax, and would have liked to cut off Vane's head before a crowd, like Charles I's. He's looking for the ax still, and probably thinks it a holy relic."

"For which reason," said Ashe, smiling, "he instantly chucked it down a well."

Paynter laughed.

"You have me there certainly," he said. "But I think you have something else in your mind. You'll say, I suppose, that we were all watching the wood; but were we? Frankly, I could almost fancy the peacock trees did strike me with a sort of sickness—a sleeping sickness."

"Well," admitted Ashe, "you have me there too. I'm afraid I couldn't swear I was awake all the time; but I don't put it down to magic trees—only to a private hobby of going to bed at night. But look here, Mr. Paynter; there's another and better argument against any outsider from the village or countryside having committed the crime. Granted he might have slipped past us somehow, and gone for the Squire. But why should he go for him in the wood? How did he know he was in the wood? You remember how suddenly the poor old boy bolted into it, on what a momentary impulse. It's the last place where one would normally look for such a man, in the middle of the night. No, it's an ugly thing to say, but we, the group round that garden table, were the only people who knew. Which brings me back to the one point in your remarks which I happen to think perfectly true."

"What was that?" inquired the other.

"That the murderer was a mystic," said Ashe. "But a cleverer mystic than poor old Martin."

Paynter made a murmur of protest, and then fell silent.

"Let us talk plainly," resumed the lawyer. "Treherne had all those mad motives you yourself admit against the woodcutter. He had the knowledge of Vane's whereabouts, which nobody can possibly attribute to the woodcutter. But he had much more. Who taunted and goaded the Squire to go into the wood at all? Treherne. Who practically prophesied, like an infernal quack astrologer, that something would happen to him if he did go into the wood? Treherne. Who was, for some reason, no matter what, obviously burning with rage and restlessness all that night, kicking his legs impatiently to and fro on the cliff, and breaking out with wild words about it being all over soon? Treherne. And on top of all this, when I walked closer to the wood, whom did I see slip out of it swiftly and silently like a shadow, but turning his face once to the moon? On my oath and on my honor—Treherne."

"It is awful," said Paynter, like a man stunned. "What you say is simply awful."

"Yes," said Ashe seriously, "very awful, but very simple. Treherne knew where the ax was originally thrown. I saw him, on that day he lunched here first, watching it like a wolf, while Miss Vane was talking to him. On that dreadful night he could easily have picked it up as he went into the wood. He knew about the well, no doubt; who was so likely to know any old traditions about the peacock trees? He hid the hat in the trees, where perhaps he hoped (though the point is unimportant) that nobody would dare to look. Anyhow, he hid it, simply because it was the one thing that would not sink in the well. Mr. Paynter, do you think I would say this of any man in mere mean dislike? Could any man say it of any man unless the case was complete, as this is complete?"

"It is complete," said Paynter, very pale. "I have nothing left against it but a faint, irrational feeling; a feeling that, somehow or other, if poor Vane could stand alive before us at this moment he might tell some other and even more incredible tale."

Ashe made a mournful gesture.

"Can these dry bones live?" he said.

"Lord Thou knowest," answered the other mechanically. "Even these dry bones—"

And he stopped suddenly with his mouth open, a blinding light of wonder in his pale eyes.

"See here," he said hoarsely and hastily. "You have said the word. What does it mean? What can it mean? Dry? Why are these bones dry?"

The lawyer started and stared down at the heap.

"Your case complete!" cried Paynter, in mounting excitement. "Where is the water in the well? The water I saw leap like a flame? Why did it leap? Where is it gone to? Complete! We are buried under riddles."

Ashe stooped, picked up a bone and looked at it.

"You are right," he said, in a low and shaken voice: "this bone is as dry—as a bone."

"Yes, I am right," replied Cyprian. "And your mystic is still as mysterious as a mystic."

There was a long silence. Ashe laid down the bone, picked up the ax and studied it more closely. Beyond the dull stain at the corner of the steel there was nothing unusual about it save a broad white rag wrapped round the handle, perhaps to give a better grip. The lawyer thought it worth noting, however, that the rag was certainly newer and cleaner than the chopper. But both were quite dry.

"Mr. Paynter," he said at last, "I admit you have scored, in the spirit if not in the letter. In strict logic, this greater puzzle is not a reply to my case. If this ax has not been dipped in water, it has been dipped in blood; and the water jumping out of the well is not an explanation of the poet jumping out of the wood. But I admit that morally and practically it does make a vital difference. We are not faced with a colossal contradiction, and we don't know how far it extends. The body might have been broken up or boiled down to its bones by the murderer, though it may be hard to connect it with the conditions of the murder. It might conceivably have been so reduced by some property in the water and soil, for decomposition varies vastly with these things. I should not dismiss my strong prima facie case against the likely person because of these difficulties. But here we have something entirely different. That the bones themselves should remain dry in a well full of water, or a well that yesterday was full of water—that brings us to the edge of something beyond which we can make no guess. There is a new factor, enormous and quite unknown. While we can't fit together such prodigious facts, we can't fit together a case against Treherne or against anybody. No; there is only one

thing to be done now. Since we can't accuse Treherne, we must appeal to him. We must put the
case against him frankly before him, and trust he
has an explanation—and will give it. I suggest we
go back and do it now."

Paynter, beginning to follow, hesitated a moment,
and then said: "Forgive me for a kind of liberty; as
you say, you are an older friend of the family. I entirely agree with your suggestion, but before you act
on your present suspicions, do you know, I think
Miss Vane ought to be warned a little? I rather fear
all this will be a new shock to her."

"Very well," said Ashe, after looking at him steadily
for an instant. "Let us go across to her first."

From the opening of the wood they could see Barbara Vane writing at the garden table, which was
littered with correspondence, and the butler with
his yellow face waiting behind her chair. As the
lengths of grass lessened between them, and the
little group at the table grew larger and clearer in
the sunlight, Paynter had a painful sense of being
part of an embassy of doom. It sharpened when
the girl looked up from the table and smiled on
seeing them.

"I should like to speak to you rather particularly if
I may," said the lawyer, with a touch of authority
in his respect; and when the butler was dismissed
he laid open the whole matter before her, speaking sympathetically, but leaving out nothing, from
the strange escape of the poet from the wood to
the last detail of the dry bones out of the well. No
fault could be found with any one of his tones or

phrases, and yet Cyprian, tingling in every nerve with the fine delicacy of his nation about the other sex, felt as if she were faced with an inquisitor. He stood about uneasily, watched the few colored clouds in the clear sky and the bright birds darting about the wood, and he heartily wished himself up the tree again.

Soon, however, the way the girl took it began to move him to perplexity rather than pity. It was like nothing he had expected, and yet he could not name the shade of difference. The final identification of her father's skull, by the hole in the hat, turned her a little pale, but left her composed; this was, perhaps, explicable, since she had from the first taken the pessimistic view. But during the rest of the tale there rested on her broad brows under her copper coils of hair, a brooding spirit that was itself a mystery. He could only tell himself that she was less merely receptive, either firmly or weakly, than he would have expected. It was as if she revolved, not their problem, but her own. She was silent a long time, and said at last:

"Thank you, Mr. Ashe, I am really very grateful for this. After all, it brings things to the point where they must have come sooner or later." She looked dreamily at the wood and sea, and went on: "I've not only had myself to consider, you see; but if you're really thinking THAT, it's time I spoke out, without asking anybody. You say, as if it were something very dreadful, 'Mr. Treherne was in the wood that night.' Well, it's not quite so dreadful to me, you see, because I know he was. In fact, we were there together."

"Together!" repeated the lawyer.

"We were together," she said quietly, "because we had a right to be together."

"Do you mean," stammered Ashe, surprised out of himself, "that you were engaged?"

"No, no," she said. "We were married."

Then, amid a startled silence, she added, as a kind of afterthought:

"In fact, we are still."

Strong as was his composure, the lawyer sat back in his chair with a sort of solid stupefaction at which Paynter could not help smiling.

"You will ask me, of course," went on Barbara in the same measured manner, "why we should be married secretly, so that even my poor father did not know. Well, I answer you quite frankly to begin with; because, if he had known, he would certainly have cut me off with a shilling. He did not like my husband, and I rather fancy you do not like him either. And when I tell you this, I know perfectly well what you will say—the usual adventurer getting hold of the usual heiress. It is quite reasonable, and, as it happens, it is quite wrong. If I had deceived my father for the sake of the money, or even for the sake of a man, I should be a little ashamed to talk to you about it. And I think you can see that I am not ashamed."

"Yes," said the American, with a grave inclination, "yes, I can see that."

She looked at him thoughtfully for a moment, as if seeking words for an obscure matter, and then said:

"Do you remember, Mr. Paynter, that day you first lunched here and told us about the African trees? Well, it was my birthday; I mean my first birthday. I was born then, or woke up or something. I had walked in this garden like a somnambulist in the sun. I think there are many such somnambulists in our set and our society; stunned with health, drugged with good manners, fitting their surroundings too well to be alive. Well, I came alive somehow; and you know how deep in us are the things we first realize when we were babies and began to take notice. I began to take notice. One of the first things I noticed was your own story, Mr. Paynter. I feel as if I heard of St. Securis as children hear of Santa Claus, and as if that big tree were a bogey I still believed in. For I do still believe in such things, or rather I believe in them more and more; I feel certain my poor father drove on the rocks by disbelieving, and you are all racing to ruin after him. That is why I do honestly want the estate, and that is why I am not ashamed of wanting it. I am perfectly certain, Mr. Paynter, that nobody can save this perishing land and this perishing people but those who understand. I mean who understand a thousand little signs and guides in the very soil and lie of the land, and traces that are almost trampled out. My husband understands, and I have begun to understand; my father would never have understood. There are powers, there is the spirit of a place, there are presences that are not to be put by. Oh, don't fancy I am sentimental and hanker after the good old days. The old days were not all good; that is just the point, and we must understand enough to know the good from the evil. We must understand enough to save the traces of a saint or a sacred tradition, or, where a wicked god has been worshiped, to destroy his altar and to cut down his grove."

"His grove," said Paynter automatically, and looked toward the little wood, where the sunbright birds were flying.

"Mrs. Treherne," said Ashe, with a formidable quietness, "I am not so unsympathetic with all this as you may perhaps suppose. I will not even say it is all moonshine, for it is something better. It is, if I may say so, honeymoonshine. I will never deny the saying that it makes the world go round, if it makes people's heads go round too. But there are other sentiments, madam, and other duties. I need not tell you your father was a good man, and that what has befallen him would be pitiable, even as the fate of the wicked. This is a horrible thing, and it is chiefly among horrors that we must keep our common sense. There are reasons for everything, and when my old friend lies butchered do not come to me with even the most beautiful fairy tales about a saint and his enchanted grove."

"Well, and you!" she cried, and rose radiantly and swiftly. "With what kind of fairy tales do you come to me? In what enchanted groves are YOU walking? You come and tell me that Mr. Paynter found a well where the water danced and then disappeared; but of course miracles are all moonshine! You tell me you yourself fished bones from under the same water, and every bone was as dry as a biscuit; but for

Heaven's sake let us say nothing that makes anybody's head go round! Really, Mr. Ashe, you must try to preserve your common sense!"

She was smiling, but with blazing eyes; and Ashe got to his feet with an involuntary laugh of surrender.

"Well, we must be going," he said. "May I say that a tribute is really due to your new transcendental training? If I may say so, I always knew you had brains; and you've been learning to use them."

The two amateur detectives went back to the wood for the moment, that Ashe might consider the removal of the unhappy Squire's remains. As he pointed out, it was now legally possible to have an inquest, and, even at that early stage of investigations, he was in favor of having it at once.

"I shall be the coroner," he said, "and I think it will be a case of 'some person or persons unknown.' Don't be surprised; it is often done to give the guilty a false security. This is not the first time the police have found it convenient to have the inquest first and the inquiry afterward."

But Paynter had paid little attention to the point; for his great gift of enthusiasm, long wasted on arts and affectations, was lifted to inspiration by the romance of real life into which he had just walked. He was really a great critic; he had a genius for admiration, and his admiration varied fittingly with everything he admired.

"A splendid girl and a splendid story," he cried. "I feel as if I were in love again myself, not so much with her as with Eve or Helen of Troy, or some such tower of beauty in the morning of the world. Don't you love all heroic things, that gravity and great candor, and the way she took one step from a sort of throne to stand in a wilderness with a vagabond? Oh, believe me, it is she who is the poet; she has the higher reason, and honor and valor are at rest in her soul."

"In short, she is uncommonly pretty," replied Ashe, with some cynicism. "I knew a murderess rather well who was very much like her, and had just that colored hair."

"You talk as if a murderer could be caught red-haired instead of red-handed," retorted Paynter. "Why, at this very minute, you could be caught red-haired yourself. Are you a murderer, by any chance?"

Ashe looked up quickly, and then smiled.

"I'm afraid I'm a connoisseur in murderers, as you are in poets," he answered, "and I assure you they are of all colors in hair as well as temperament. I suppose it's inhumane, but mine is a monstrously interesting trade, even in a little place like this. As for that girl, of course I've known her all her life, and—but—but that is just the question. Have I known her all her life? Have I known her at all? Was she even there to be known? You admire her for telling the truth; and so she did, by God, when she said that some people wake up late, who have never lived before. Do we know what they might do—we, who have only seen them asleep?"

"Great heavens!" cried Paynter. "You don't dare suggest that she—"

"No, I don't," said the lawyer, with composure, "but there are other reasons.... I don't suggest anything fully, till we've had our interview with this poet of yours. I think I know where to find him."

They found him, in fact, before they expected him, sitting on the bench outside the Vane Arms, drinking a mug of cider and waiting for the return of his American friend; so it was not difficult to open conversation with him. Nor did he in any way avoid the subject of the tragedy; and the lawyer, seating himself also on the long bench that fronted the little market place, was soon putting the last developments as lucidly as he had put them to Barbara.

"Well," said Treherne at last, leaning back and frowning at the signboard, with the colored birds and dolphins, just about his head; "suppose somebody did kill the Squire. He'd killed a good many people with his hygiene and his enlightened landlordism."

Paynter was considerably uneasy at this alarming opening; but the poet went on quite coolly, with his hands in his pockets and his feet thrust out into the street.

"When a man has the power of a Sultan in Turkey, and uses it with the ideas of a spinster in Tooting, I often wonder that nobody puts a knife in him. I wish there were more sympathy for murderers, somehow. I'm very sorry the poor old fellow's gone myself; but you gentlemen always seem to forget there are any other people in the world. He's all right; he was a good fellow, and his soul, I fancy, has gone to the happiest paradise of all."

The anxious American could read nothing of the effect of this in the dark Napoleonic face of the lawyer, who merely said: "What do you mean?"

"The fool's paradise," said Treherne, and drained his pot of cider.

The lawyer rose. He did not look at Treherne, or speak to him; but looked and spoke straight across him to the American, who found the utterance not a little unexpected.

"Mr. Paynter," said Ashe, "you thought it rather morbid of me to collect murderers; but it's fortunate for your own view of the case that I do. It may surprise you to know that Mr. Treherne has now, in my eyes, entirely cleared himself of suspicion. I have been intimate with several assassins, as I remarked; but there's one thing none of them ever did. I never knew a murderer to talk about the murder, and then at once deny it and defend it. No, if a man is concealing his crime, why should he go out of his way to apologize for it?"

"Well," said Paynter, with his ready appreciation, "I always said you were a remarkable man; and that's certainly a remarkable idea."

"Do I understand," asked the poet, kicking his heels on the cobbles, "that both you gentlemen have been kindly directing me toward the gallows?"

"No," said Paynter thoughtfully. "I never thought you guilty; and even supposing I had, if you understand me, I should never have thought it quite so guilty to be guilty. It would not have been for money or any mean thing, but for something a little wilder and worthier of a man of genius. After all, I suppose, the poet has passions like great unearthly appetites; and the world has always judged more gently of his sins. But now that Mr. Ashe admits your innocence, I can honestly say I have always affirmed it."

The poet rose also. "Well, I am innocent, oddly enough," he said. "I think I can make a guess about your vanishing well, but of the death and dry bones I know no more than the dead; if so much. And, by the way, my dear Paynter"—and he turned two bright eyes on the art critic—"I will excuse you from excusing me for all the things I haven't done; and you, I hope, will excuse me if I differ from you altogether about the morality of poets. As you suggest, it is a fashionable view, but I think it is a fallacy. No man has less right to be lawless than a man of imagination. For he has spiritual adventures, and can take his holidays when he likes. I could picture the poor Squire carried off to elfland whenever I wanted him carried off, and that wood needed no crime to make it wicked for me. That red sunset the other night was all that a murder would have been to many men. No, Mr. Ashe; show, when next you sit in judgment, a little mercy to some wretched man who drinks and robs because he must drink beer to taste it, and take it to drink it. Have compassion on the next batch of poor thieves, who have to hold things in order to have them. But if ever you find *me* stealing one small farthing, when I can shut my eyes and see the city of El Dorado, then"—and he lifted his head like a falcon—"show me no mercy, for I shall deserve none."

"Well," remarked Ashe, after a pause, "I must go and fix things up for the inquest. Mr. Treherne, your attitude is singularly interesting; I really almost wish I could add you to my collection of murderers. They are a varied and extraordinary set."

"Has it ever occurred to you," asked Paynter, "that perhaps the men who have never committed murder are a varied and very extraordinary set? Perhaps every plain man's life holds the real mystery, the secret of sins avoided."

"Possibly," replied Ashe. "It would be a long business to stop the next man in the street and ask him what crimes he never committed and why not. And I happen to be busy, so you'll excuse me."

"What," asked the American, when he and the poet were alone, "is this guess of yours about the vanishing water?"

"Well, I'm not sure I'll tell you yet," answered Treherne, something of the old mischief coming back into his dark eyes. "But I'll tell you something else, which may be connected with it; something I couldn't tell until my wife had told you about our meeting in the wood." His face had grown grave again, and he resumed after a pause:

"When my wife started to follow her father I advised her to go back first to the house, to leave it by another door and to meet me in the wood in half an hour. We often made these assignations, of course, and generally thought them great fun, but this time the question was serious, and I didn't want the wrong thing done in a hurry. It was a question whether anything could be done to undo an experiment we both vaguely felt to be dangerous, and she especially thought, after reflection, that interference would make things worse. She thought the old sportsman, having been dared to do something, would certainly not be dissuaded by the very man who had dared him or by a woman whom he regarded as a child. She left me at last in a sort of despair, but I lingered with a last hope of doing something, and drew doubtfully near to the heart of the wood; and there, instead of the silence I expected, I heard a voice. It seemed as if the Squire must be talking to himself, and I had the unpleasant fancy that he had already lost his reason in that wood of witchcraft. But I soon found that if he was talking he was talking with two voices. Other fancies attacked me, as that the other was the voice of the tree or the voices of the three trees talking together, and with no man near. But it was not the voice of the tree. The next moment I knew the voice, for I had heard it twenty times across the table. It was the voice of that doctor of yours; I heard it as certainly as you hear my voice now."

After a moment's silence, he resumed: "I left the wood, I hardly knew why, and with wild and bewildered feelings; and as I came out into the faint moonshine I saw that old lawyer standing quietly, but staring at me like an owl. At least, the light touched his red hair with fire, but his square old face was in shadow. But I knew, if I could have read it, that it was the face of a hanging judge."

He threw himself on the bench again, smiled a little, and added: "Only, like a good many hanging judges, I fancy, he was waiting patiently to hang the wrong man."

"And the right man—" said Paynter mechanically. Treherne shrugged his shoulders, sprawling on the ale bench, and played with his empty pot.

IV. THE CHASE AFTER THE TRUTH

Some time after the inquest, which had ended in the inconclusive verdict which Mr. Andrew Ashe had himself predicted and achieved, Paynter was again sitting on the bench outside the village inn, having on the little table in front of it a tall glass of light ale, which he enjoyed much more as local color than as liquor. He had but one companion on the bench, and that a new one, for the little market place was empty at that hour, and he had lately, for the rest, been much alone. He was not unhappy, for he resembled his great countryman, Walt Whitman, in carrying a kind of universe with him like an open umbrella; but he was not only alone, but lonely. For Ashe had gone abruptly up to London, and since his return had been occupied obscurely with legal matters, doubtless bearing on the murder. And Treherne had long since taken up his position openly, at the great house, as the husband of the great lady, and he and she were occupied with sweeping reforms on the estate. The lady especially, being of the sort whose very dreams "drive at practice," was landscape gardening as with the gestures of a giantess. It was natural, therefore, that so sociable a spirit as Paynter should fall into speech with the one other stranger who happened to be staying at the inn, evidently a bird of passage like himself. This man, who was smoking a pipe on the bench beside him, with his knapsack before him on the table, was an artist come to sketch on that romantic coast; a tall man in a velvet jacket, with a shock of tow-colored hair, a long fair beard, but eyes of dark brown, the effect of which contrast reminded Paynter vaguely, he hardly knew why, of a Russian. The stranger carried his knapsack into many picturesque corners; he obtained permission to set up his easel in that high garden where the late Squire had held his al fresco banquets. But Paynter had never had an opportunity of judging of the artist's work, nor did he find it easy to get the artist even to talk of his art. Cyprian himself was always ready to talk of any art, and he talked of it excellently, but with little response. He gave his own reasons for preferring the Cubists to the cult of Picasso, but his new friend seemed to have but a faint interest in either. He insinuated that perhaps the Neo-Primitives were after all only thinning their line, while the true Primitives were rather tightening it; but the stranger seemed to receive the insinuation without any marked reaction of feeling. When Paynter had even gone back as far into the past as the Post-Impressionists to find a common ground, and not found it, other memories began to creep back into his mind. He was just reflecting, rather darkly, that after all the tale of the peacock trees needed a mysterious stranger to round it off, and this man had much the air of being one, when the mysterious stranger himself said suddenly:

"Well, I think I'd better show you the work I'm doing down here."

He had his knapsack before him on the table, and he smiled rather grimly as he began to unstrap it. Paynter looked on with polite expressions of interest, but was considerably surprised when the artist unpacked and placed on the table, not any recognizable works of art, even of the most Cubist description, but (first) a quire of foolscap closely written with notes in black and red ink, and (second), to the American's extreme amazement, the old woodman's ax with the linen wrapper, which he had himself found in the well long ago.

"Sorry to give you a start, sir," said the Russian artist, with a marked London accent. "But I'd better explain straight off that I'm a policeman."

"You don't look it," said Paynter.

"I'm not supposed to," replied the other. "Mr. Ashe brought me down here from the Yard to investigate; but he told me to report to you when I'd got anything to go on. Would you like to go into the matter now?

"When I took this matter up," explained the detective, "I did it at Mr. Ashe's request, and largely, of course, on Mr. Ashe's lines. Mr. Ashe is a great criminal lawyer; with a beautiful brain, sir, as full as the Newgate Calendar. I took, as a working notion, his view that only you five gentlemen round the table in the Squire's garden were acquainted with the Squire's movements. But you gentlemen, if I may say so, have a way of forgetting certain other things and other people which we are rather taught to look for first. And as I followed Mr. Ashe's inquiries through the stages you know already, through certain suspicions I needn't discuss because they've been dropped, I found the thing shaping after all toward something, in the end, which I think we should have considered at the beginning. Now, to begin with, it is not true that there were five men round the table. There were six."

The creepy conditions of that garden vigil vaguely returned upon Paynter; and he thought of a ghost, or something more nameless than a ghost. But the deliberate speech of the detective soon enlightened him.

"There were six men and five gentlemen, if you like to put it so," he proceeded. "That man Miles, the butler, saw the Squire vanish as plainly as you did; and I soon found that Miles was a man worthy of a good deal of attention."

A light of understanding dawned on Paynter's face. "So that was it, was it!" he muttered.

"Does all our mythological mystery end with a policeman collaring a butler? Well, I agree with you he is far from an ordinary butler, even to look at; and the fault in imagination is mine. Like many faults in imagination, it was simply snobbishness."

"We don't go quite so fast as that," observed the officer, in an impassive manner. "I only said I found the inquiry pointing to Miles; and that he was well worthy of attention. He was much more in the old Squire's confidence than many people supposed; and when I cross-examined him he told me a good deal that was worth knowing. I've got it all down in these notes here; but at the moment I'll only trouble you with one detail of it. One night this butler was just outside the Squire's dining-room door, when he heard the noise of a violent quarrel. The Squire was a violent gentleman, from time to time; but the curious thing about this scene was that the other gentleman was the more violent of the two. Miles heard him say repeatedly that the Squire was a public nuisance, and that his death would be a good riddance for everybody. I only stop now to tell you that the other gentleman was Dr. Burton Brown, the medical man of this village.

"The next examination I made was that of Martin, the woodcutter. Upon one point at least his evidence is quite clear, and is, as you will see, largely confirmed by other witnesses. He says first that the doctor prevented him from recovering his ax, and this is corroborated by Mr. and Mrs. Treherne. But he says further that the doctor admitted having the thing himself; and this again finds support in other evidence by the gardener, who saw the doctor, some time afterward, come by himself and pick up the chopper. Martin says that Doctor Brown repeatedly refused to give it up, alleging some fanciful excuse every time. And, finally, Mr. Paynter, we will hear the evidence of the ax itself."

He laid the woodman's tool on the table in front of him, and began to rip up and unwrap the curious linen covering round the handle.

"You will admit this is an odd bandage," he said. "And that's just the odd thing about it, that it really is a bandage. This white stuff is the sort of lint they use in hospitals, cut into strips like this. But most doctors keep some; and I have the evidence of Jake the fisherman, with whom Doctor Brown lived for some time, that the doctor had this useful habit. And, last," he added, flattening out a corner of the rag on the table, "isn't it odd that it should be marked T.B.B.?"

The American gazed at the rudely inked initials, but hardly saw them. What he saw, as in a mirror in his darkened memory, was the black figure with the black gloves against the blood-red sunset, as he had seen it when he came out of the wood, and which had always haunted him, he knew not why.

"Of course, I see what you mean," he said, "and it's very painful for me, for I knew and respected the man. But surely, also, it's very far from explaining everything. If he is a murderer, is he a magician? Why did the well water all evaporate in a night, and leave the dead man's bones dry as dust? That's not a common operation in the hospitals, is it?"

"As to the water, we do know the explanation," said the detective. "I didn't tumble to it at first myself, being a Cockney; but a little talk with Jake and the other fisherman about the old smuggling days put me straight about that. But I admit the dried remains still stump us all. All the same—"

A shadow fell across the table, and his talk was sharply cut short. Ashe was standing under the painted sign, buttoned up grimly in black, and with the face of the hanging judge, of which the poet had spoken, plain this time in the broad sunlight. Behind him stood two big men in plain clothes, very still; but Paynter knew instantly who they were.

"We must move at once," said the lawyer. "Dr. Burton Brown is leaving the village."

The tall detective sprang to his feet, and Paynter instinctively imitated him.

"He has gone up to the Trehernes possibly to say good-by," went on Ashe rapidly. "I'm sorry, but we must arrest him in the garden there, if necessary. I've kept the lady out of the way, I think. But you"—addressing the factitious landscape painter—"must go up at once and rig up that easel of yours near the table and be ready. We will follow quietly, and come up behind the tree. We must be careful, for it's clear he's got wind of us, or he wouldn't be doing a bolt."

"I don't like this job," remarked Paynter, as they mounted toward the park and garden, the detective darting on ahead.

"Do you suppose I do?" asked Ashe; and, indeed, his strong, heavy face looked so lined and old that the red hair seemed unnatural, like a red wig. "I've known him longer than you, though perhaps I've suspected him longer as well."

When they topped the slope of the garden the detective had already erected his easel, though a strong breeze blowing toward the sea rattled and flapped his apparatus and blew about his fair (and false) beard in the wind. Little clouds curled like feathers, were scudding seaward across the many-colored landscape, which the American art critic had once surveyed on a happier morning; but it is doubtful if the landscape painter paid much attention to it. Treherne was dimly discernible in the doorway of what was now his house; he would come no nearer, for he hated such a public duty more bitterly than the rest. The others posted themselves a little way behind the tree. Between the lines of these masked batteries the black figure of the doctor could be seen coming across the green lawn, traveling straight, as a bullet, as he had done when he brought the bad news to the woodcutter. To-day he was smiling, under the dark mustache that was cut short of the upper lip, though they fancied him a little pale, and he seemed to pause a moment and peer through his spectacles at the artist.

The artist turned from his easel with a natural movement, and then in a flash had captured the doctor by the coat collar.

"I arrest you—" he began; but Doctor Brown plucked himself free with startling promptitude, took a flying leap at the other, tore off his sham beard, tossing it into the air like one of the wild wisps of the cloud; then, with one wild kick, sent the easel flying topsy-turvy, and fled like a hare for the shore. Even at that dazzling instant Paynter felt that this wild reception was a novelty and almost an anticlimax; but he had no time for analysis when he and the whole pack had to follow in the hunt; even Treherne bringing up the rear with a renewed curiosity and energy.

The fugitive collided with one of the policemen who ran to head him off, sending him sprawling down the slope; indeed, the fugitive seemed inspired with the strength of a wild ape. He cleared at a bound the rampart of flowers, over which Barbara had once leaned to look at her future lover, and tumbled with blinding speed down the steep path up which that troubadour had climbed. Racing with the rushing wind they all streamed across the garden after him, down the path, and finally on to the seashore by the fisher's cot, and the pierced crags and caverns the American had admired when he first landed. The runaway did not, however, make for the house he had long inhabited, but rather for the pier, as if with a mind to seize the boat or to swim. Only when he reached the other end of the small stone jetty did he turn, and show them the pale face with the spectacles; and they saw that it was still smiling.

"I'm rather glad of this," said Treherne, with a great sigh. "The man is mad."

Nevertheless, the naturalness of the doctor's voice, when he spoke, startled them as much as a shriek.

"Gentleman," he said, "I won't protract your painful duties by asking you what you want; but I will ask at once for a small favor, which will not prejudice those duties in any way. I came down here rather in a hurry perhaps; but the truth is I thought I was late for an appointment." He looked dispassionately at his watch. "I find there is still some fifteen minutes. Will you wait with me here for that short time; after which I am quite at your service."

There was a bewildered silence, and then Paynter said: "For my part, I feel as if it would really be better to humor him."

"Ashe," said the doctor, with a new note of seriousness, "for old friendship, grant me this last little
indulgence. It will make no difference; I have no
arms or means of escape; you can search me if you
like. I know you think you are doing right, and I
also know you will do it as fairly as you can. Well,
after all, you get friends to help you; look at our
friend with the beard, or the remains of the beard.
Why shouldn't I have a friend to help me? A man
will be here in a few minutes in whom I put some
confidence; a great authority on these things. Why
not, if only out of curiosity, wait and hear his view
of the case?"

"This seems all moonshine," said Ashe, "but on
the chance of any light on things—well, from the
moon—I don't mind waiting a quarter of an hour.
Who is this friend, I wonder; some amateur detective, I suppose."

"I thank you," said the doctor, with some dignity.
"I think you will trust him when you have talked to
him a little. And now," he added with an air of ami-
ably relaxing into lighter matters, "let us talk about
the murder.

"This case," he said in a detached manner, "will
be found, I suspect, to be rather unique. There is a
very clear and conclusive combination of evidence
against Thomas Burton Brown, otherwise myself.
But there is one peculiarity about that evidence,
which you may perhaps have noticed. It all comes
ultimately from one source, and that a rather unusual one. Thus, the woodcutter says I had his ax,
but what makes him think so? He says I told him I
had his ax; that I told him so again and again. Once

more, Mr. Paynter here pulled up the ax out of the well; but how? I think Mr. Paynter will testify that I brought him the tackle for fishing it up, tackle he might never have got in any other way. Curious, is it not? Again, the ax is found to be wrapped in lint that was in my possession, according to the fisherman. But who showed the lint to the fisherman? I did. Who marked it with large letters as mine? I did. Who wrapped it round the handle at all? I did. Rather a singular thing to do; has anyone ever explained it?"

His words, which had been heard at first with painful coldness were beginning to hold more and more of their attention.

"Then there is the well itself," proceeded the doctor, with the same air of insane calm. "I suppose some of you by this time know at least the secret of that. The secret of the well is simply that it is not a well. It is purposely shaped at the top so as to look like one, but it is really a sort of chimney opening from the roof of one of those caves over there; a cave that runs inland just under the wood, and indeed IS connected by tunnels and secret passages with other openings miles and miles away. It is a sort of labyrinth used by smugglers and such people for ages past. This doubtless explains many of those disappearances we have heard of. But to return to the well that is not a well, in case some of you still don't know about it. When the sea rises very high at certain seasons it fills the low cave, and even rises a little way in the funnel above, making it look more like a well than ever. The noise Mr. Paynter heard was the natural eddy of a breaker from outside, and the whole experience depended on something so elementary as the tide."

The American was startled into ordinary speech.

"The tide!" he said. "And I never even thought of it! I guess that comes of living by the Mediterranean."

"The next step will be obvious enough," continued the speaker, "to a logical mind like that of Mr. Ashe, for instance. If it be asked why, even so, the tide did not wash away the Squire's remains that had lain there since his disappearance, there is only one possible answer. The remains had *not* lain there since his disappearance. The remains had been deliberately put there in the cavern under the wood, and put there *after* Mr. Paynter had made his first investigation. They were put there, in short, after the sea had retreated and the cave was again dry. That is why they were dry; of course, much drier than the cave. Who put them there, I wonder?"

He was gazing gravely through his spectacles over their heads into vacancy, and suddenly he smiled.

"Ah," he cried, jumping up from the rock with alacrity, "here is the amateur detective at last!"

Ashe turned his head over his shoulder, and for a few seconds did not move it again, but stood as if with a stiff neck. In the cliff just behind him was one of the clefts or cracks into which it was everywhere cloven. Advancing from this into the sunshine, as if from a narrow door, was Squire Vane, with a broad smile on his face.

The wind was tearing from the top of the high cliff out to sea, passing over their heads, and they had the sensation that everything was passing over their heads and out of their control. Paynter felt as if his head had been blown off like a hat. But none of this gale of unreason seemed to stir a hair on the white head of the Squire, whose bearing, though self-important and bordering on a swagger, seemed if anything more comfortable than in the old days. His red face was, however, burnt like a sailor's, and his light clothes had a foreign look.

"Well, gentlemen," he said genially, "so this is the end of the legend of the peacock trees. Sorry to spoil that delightful traveler's tale, Mr. Paynter, but the joke couldn't be kept up forever. Sorry to put a stop to your best poem, Mr. Treherne, but I thought all this poetry had been going a little too far. So Doctor Brown and I fixed up a little surprise for you. And I must say, without vanity, that you look a little surprised."

"What on earth," asked Ashe at last, "is the meaning of all this?"

The Squire laughed pleasantly, and even a little apologetically,

"I'm afraid I'm fond of practical jokes," he said, "and this I suppose is my last grand practical joke. But I want you to understand that the joke is really practical. I flatter myself it will be of very practical use to the cause of progress and common sense, and the killing of such superstitions everywhere. The best part of it, I admit, was the doctor's idea and not mine. All I meant to do was to pass a night in the trees, and then turn up as fresh as paint to tell you what fools you were. But Doctor Brown here followed me into the wood, and we had a little talk which rather changed my plans. He told me that a disappearance for a few hours like that would never knock the nonsense on the head; most people would never even hear of it, and those who did would say that one night proved nothing. He showed me a much better way, which had been tried in several cases where bogus miracles had been shown up. The thing to do was to get the thing really believed everywhere as a miracle, and then shown up everywhere as a sham miracle. I can't put all the arguments as well as he did, but that was the notion, I think."

The doctor nodded, gazing silently at the sand; and the Squire resumed with undiminished relish.

"We agreed that I should drop through the hole into the cave, and make my way through the tunnels, where I often used to play as a boy, to the railway station a few miles from here, and there take a train for London. It was necessary for the joke, of course, that I should disappear without being traced; so I made my way to a port, and put in a very pleasant month or two round my old haunts in Cyprus and the Mediterranean. There's no more to say of that part of the business, except that I arranged to be back by a particular time; and here I am. But I've heard enough of what's gone on round here to be satisfied that I've done the trick. Everybody in Cornwall and most people in South England have heard of the Vanishing Squire; and thousands of noodles have been nodding their heads over crystals and tarot cards at this marvelous proof of an unseen world. I reckon the Reappearing Squire will scatter their cards and smash their crystals, so that such rubbish won't appear again in the twentieth century. I'll make the peacock trees the laughing stock of all Europe and America."

"Well," said the lawyer, who was the first to rearrange his wits, "I'm sure we're all only too delighted to see you again, Squire; and I quite understand your explanation and your own very natural motives in the matter. But I'm afraid I haven't got the hang of everything yet. Granted that you wanted to vanish, was it necessary to put bogus bones in the cave, so as nearly to put a halter round the neck of Doctor Brown? And who put it there? The statement would appear perfectly maniacal; but so far as I can make head or tail out of anything, Doctor Brown seems to have put it there himself."

The doctor lifted his head for the first time.

"Yes; I put the bones there," he said. "I believe I am the first son of Adam who ever manufactured all the evidence of a murder charge against himself."

It was the Squire's turn to look astonished. The old gentleman looked rather wildly from one to the other.

"Bones! Murder charge!" he ejaculated. "What the devil is all this? Whose bones?"

"Your bones, in a manner of speaking," delicately conceded the doctor. "I had to make sure you had really died, and not disappeared by magic."

The Squire in his turn seemed more hopelessly puzzled than the whole crowd of his friends had been over his own escapade. "Why not?" he demanded. "I thought it was the whole point to make it look like magic. Why did you want me to die so much?"

Doctor Brown had lifted his head; and he now very slowly lifted his hand. He pointed with outstretched arm at the headland overhanging the foreshore, just above the entrance to the cave. It was the exact part of the beach where Paynter had first landed, on that spring morning when he had looked up in his first fresh wonder at the peacock trees. But the trees were gone.

The fact itself was no surprise to them; the clearance had naturally been one of the first of the sweeping changes of the Treherne regime. But though they knew it well, they had wholly forgotten it; and its significance returned on them suddenly like a sign in heaven.

"That is the reason," said the doctor. "I have worked for that for fourteen years."

They no longer looked at the bare promontory on which the feathery trees had once been so familiar a sight; for they had something else to look at. Anyone seeing the Squire now would have shifted his opinion about where to find the lunatic in that crowd. It was plain in a flash that the change had fallen on him like a thunderbolt; that he, at least, had never had the wildest notion that the tale of the Vanishing Squire had been but a prelude to that of the vanishing trees. The next half hour was full of his ravings and expostulations, which gradually died away into demands for explanation and incoherent questions repeated again and again. He had practically to be overruled at last, in spite of the respect in which he was held, before anything like a space and silence were made in which the doctor could tell his own story. It was perhaps a singular story, of which he alone had ever had the knowledge; and though its narration was not uninterrupted, it may be set forth consecutively in his own words.

"First, I wish it clearly understood that I believe in nothing. I do not even give the nothing I believe a name; or I should be an atheist. I have never had inside my head so much as a hint of heaven and hell. I think it most likely we are worms in the mud; but I happen to be sorry for the other worms under the wheel. And I happen myself to be a sort of worm that turns when he can. If I care nothing for piety, I care less for poetry. I'm not like Ashe here, who is crammed with criminology, but has all sorts of other culture as well. I know nothing about culture, except bacteria culture. I sometimes fancy Mr. Ashe is as much an art critic as Mr. Paynter; only he looks for his heroes, or villains, in real life. But I am a very practical man; and my stepping stones have been simply scientific facts. In this village I found a fact—a fever. I could not classify it; it seemed peculiar to this corner of the coast; it had singular reactions of delirium and mental breakdown. I studied it exactly as I should a queer case in the hospital, and corresponded and compared notes with other men of science. But nobody had even a working hypothesis about it, except of course the ignorant peasantry, who said the peacock trees were in some wild way poisonous.

"Well, the peacock trees were poisonous. The peacock trees did produce the fever. I verified the fact in the plain plodding way required, comparing all the degrees and details of a vast number of cases; and there were a shocking number to compare. At the end of it I had discovered the thing as Harvey discovered the circulation of the blood. Everybody was the worse for being near the things; those who came off best were exactly the exceptions that proved the rule, abnormally healthy and energetic people like the Squire and his daughter. In other words, the peasants were right. But if I put it that way, somebody will cry: 'But do you believe it was supernatural then?' In fact, that's what you'll all say; and that's exactly what I complain of. I fancy hundreds of men have been left dead and diseases left undiscovered, by this suspicion of superstition, this stupid fear of fear. Unless you see daylight through the forest of facts from the first, you won't venture into the wood at all. Unless we can promise you beforehand that there shall be what you call a natural explanation, to save your precious dignity from miracles, you won't even hear the beginning of the plain tale. Suppose there isn't a natural explanation! Suppose there is, and we never find it! Suppose I haven't a notion whether there is or not! What the devil has that to do with you, or with me in dealing with the facts I do know? My own instinct is to think there is; that if my researches could be followed far enough it would be found that some horrible parody of hay fever, some effect analogous to that of pollen, would explain all the facts. I have never found the explanation. What I have found are the facts. And the fact is that those trees on the top there dealt death right and left, as certainly as if they had been giants, standing on a hill and knocking men down in crowds with a club. It will be said that now I had only to produce my proofs and have the nuisance removed. Perhaps I might have convinced the scientific world finally, when more and more processions of dead men had passed through the village to the cemetery. But I had not got to convince the scientific world, but the Lord of the Manor. The Squire will pardon my saying that it was a very different thing. I tried it once; I lost my temper, and said things I do not defend; and I left the Squire's prejudices rooted anew, like the trees. I was confronted with one colossal coincidence that was an obstacle to all my aims. One thing made all my science sound like nonsense. It was the popular legend.

"Squire, if there were a legend of hay fever, you would not believe in hay fever. If there were a popular story about pollen, you would say that pollen was only a popular story. I had something against me heavier and more hopeless than the hostility of the learned; I had the support of the ignorant. My truth was hopelessly tangled up with a tale that the educated were resolved to regard as entirely a lie. I never tried to explain again; on the contrary, I apologized, affected a conversion to the common-sense view, and watched events. And all the time the lines of a larger, if more crooked plan, began to get clearer in my mind. I knew that Miss Vane, whether or no she were married to Mr. Treherne, as I afterward found she was, was so much under his influence that the first day of her inheritance would be the last day of the poisonous trees. But she could not inherit, or even interfere, till the Squire died. It became simply self-evident, to a rational mind, that the Squire must die. But wishing to be humane as well as rational, I desired his death to be temporary.

"Doubtless my scheme was completed by a chapter of accidents, but I was watching for such accidents. Thus I had a foreshadowing of how the ax would figure in the tale when it was first flung at the trees; it would have surprised the woodman to know how near our minds were, and how I was but laying a more elaborate siege to the towers of pestilence. But when the Squire spontaneously rushed on what half the countryside would call certain death, I jumped at my chance. I followed him, and told him all that he has told you. I don't suppose he'll ever forgive me now, but that shan't prevent me saying that I admire him hugely for being what people would call a lunatic and what is really a sportsman. It takes rather a grand old man to make a joke in the grand style. He came down so quick from the tree he had climbed that he had no time to pull his hat off the bough it had caught in.

"At first I found I had made a miscalculation. I thought his disappearance would be taken as his death, at least after a little time; but Ashe told me there could be no formalities without a corpse. I fear I was a little annoyed, but I soon set myself to the duty of manufacturing a corpse. It's not hard for a doctor to get a skeleton; indeed, I had one, but Mr. Paynter's energy was a day too early for me, and I only got the bones into the well when he had already found it. His story gave me another chance, however; I noted where the hole was in the hat, and made a precisely corresponding hole in the skull. The reason for creating the other clews may not be so obvious. It may not yet be altogether apparent to you that I am not a fiend in human form. I could not substantiate a murder without at least suggesting a murderer, and I was resolved that if the crime happened to be traced to anybody, it should be to me. So I'm not surprised you were puzzled about the purpose of the rag round the ax, because it had no purpose, except to incriminate the man who put it there. The chase had to end with me, and when it was closing in at last the joke of it was too much for me, and I fear I took liberties with the gentleman's easel and beard. I was the only person who could risk it, being the only person who could at the last moment produce the Squire and prove there had been no crime at all. That, gentlemen, is the true story of the peacock trees; and that bare crag up there, where the wind is whistling as it would over a wilderness, is a waste place I have labored to make, as many men have labored to make a cathedral.

"I don't think there is any more to say, and yet something moves in my blood and I will try to say it. Could you not have trusted a little these peasants whom you already trust so much? These men are men, and they meant something; even their fathers were not wholly fools. If your gardener told you of the trees you called him a madman, but he did not plan and plant your garden like a madman. You would not trust your woodman about these trees, yet you trusted him with all the others. Have you ever thought what all the work of the world would be like if the poor were so senseless as you think them? But no, you stuck to your rational principle. And your rational principle was that a thing must be false because thousands of men had found it true; that *because* many human eyes had seen something it could not be there."

He looked across at Ashe with a sort of challenge, but though the sea wind ruffled the old lawyer's red mane, his Napoleonic mask was unruffled; it even had a sort of beauty from its new benignity.

"I am too happy just now in thinking how wrong I have been," he answered, "to quarrel with you, doctor, about our theories. And yet, in justice to the Squire as well as myself, I should demur to your sweeping inference. I respect these peasants, I respect your regard for them; but their stories are a different matter. I think I would do anything for them but believe them. Truth and fancy, after all, are mixed in them, when in the more instructed they are separate; and I doubt if you have considered what would be involved in taking their word for anything. Half the ghosts of those who died of fever may be walking by now; and kind as these people are, I believe they might still burn a witch. No, doctor, I admit these people have been badly used, I admit they are in many ways our betters, but I still could not accept anything in their evidence."

The doctor bowed gravely and respectfully enough, and then, for the last time that day, they saw his rather sinister smile.

"Quite so," he said. "But you would have hanged me on their evidence."

And, turning his back on them, as if automatically, he set his face toward the village, where for so many years he had gone his round.